# The Resurrection of Knox Martin

Allen Sircy

Published by Southern Ghost Stories, Gallatin, Tennessee

ISBN: 979-8-9988146-2-4

# Table of Contents

# Prologue

In 1780, Italian physician Luigi Galvani discovered that a dead frog's legs could twitch with the touch of metal and a jolt of electricity. He believed he had uncovered the key to "animal electricity" — a vital spark that animated all living creatures. Though crude and misunderstood, the experiments of Galvani and his nephew Giovanni Aldini opened a doorway. Behind it lay not just science, but something older and darker: man's desire to control life and death.

The world took notice.

By January 1, 1818, *Frankenstein; or The Modern Prometheus* was published anonymously in London. Its 19-year-old author, Mary Shelley, imagined the tragic tale of Victor Frankenstein, a young scientist who gathered the remnants of the dead and used galvanic forces to reanimate a towering, intelligent Creature — a being rejected by its creator and feared by the world. Though fictional, Shelley's story was steeped in contemporary debates on science, morality, and resurrection.

Later that same year, on October 3, 1818, Scottish surgeon Dr. Andrew Ure conducted a real and shocking public demonstration in Glasgow. The subject was Matthew Clydesdale, a convicted murderer who had recently been hanged. Before a crowd, Ure applied electrodes to the corpse's chest and jaw. The dead man's eyes flared open. His diaphragm convulsed. One arm raised. Some in the audience fainted. Others claimed to have heard a groan.

As galvanic fever crossed the Atlantic, similar experiments soon emerged across the United States, often in secrecy, sometimes in full view. From Sherman, Connecticut to St. Louis, Missouri... from Chicago, Illinois to Columbus, Ohio... Louisville, Kentucky, Knoxville, Tennessee, Franklin, Tennessee, and Huntsville, Alabama—all bore witness to mankind's desire to master death with wire, copper, and current.

But none of these cases would match the bizarre, public, and unsolved events that unfolded in Nashville, Tennessee in the spring of 1879.

There, a man named Knox Martin was convicted of a brutal double homicide, hanged by the neck until dead, and carted away under cover of night to the Nashville Medical College. What happened in the hours that followed would become a national scandal, whispered in courtrooms, saloons, and Sunday sermons for decades. According to some, Knox Martin rose again.

# The Offer

It was late 1878, and the chill in the air was sharp as John Whittemeyer walked through the door of the general store on the outskirts of Nashville. He carried himself with the air of a wealthy farmer accustomed to getting what he wanted. His boots scraped against the wooden floor as he stepped inside, his eyes scanning the shelves with a look of confusion. Whatever he was looking for, he couldn't find it.

Perry Cowan, the store's friendly owner saw John's puzzled look and approached him with a warm smile.

"Good morning, John. It's good to see you," Perry greeted, placing some bundles of twine on the counter.

John glanced at him, frowning slightly. "I see you've moved things around. Where are you hiding the molasses?"

Perry chuckled, leading John toward the back of the store. "It's right over here. I changed things around about a month ago. I haven't seen you in a while. Where've you been?"

John shrugged, his eyes shifting towards the shelves as he followed Perry. "Big John hurt his back and went back home. It's just me and Emily trying to keep up with the farm. You know anyone looking for work?"

Perry glanced across the room, nodding toward the young African-American man stacking jars on a counter. "I've got a fellow I hired a few months ago. Things have been slow with this cold weather. I've been thinking about letting him go."

John's attention shifted toward the young man, who was unassuming yet strong. Knox Martin, 25 years old, was quietly going about his work, stacking the jars with a methodical precision that caught John's eye.

"You really been thinking about letting him go?" John asked curiously.

"Until the weather turns, I don't have much for him to do," Perry replied. "No one's buying much these days. He works hard and is reliable, though. If you need help around the farm, go talk to him."

John studied Knox, a thought forming in his mind. He then walked over, extending a hand. "Good morning. I'm John Whittemeyer. What's your name?"

Knox looked up from his task and offered a polite smile. "Morning, sir. I'm Knox."

John gave him a quick once-over. "I'm looking for some help on my farm, and Perry tells me you're a good worker. I could make it worth your while."

Knox raised an eyebrow, intrigued. "What kind of work?"

"I live right across Bell's Bend. We've got thirty acres. What kind of experience do you have? Have you worked on a farm that big before?"

Knox nodded, his gaze steady. "Yes, sir. Worked on a plantation in Jackson County, Alabama, before the war. When I got to Nashville, I worked for George Berry at a livery stable downtown for a bit, handling horses and wagons."

John nodded thoughtfully. "Well, I can pay twelve dollars a week if you're interested. If you agree to stay on for a year, I can increase it to fifteen and let you stay in a cabin on the property."

Knox hesitated, his expression revealing some uncertainty. But the offer was tempting, and something in his chest stirred at the idea of a better future.

"I'll be honest with you," John continued, "right now there's not much to do, but come March, when the weather breaks, the days will get long."

Knox paused, turning his head toward Perry for a moment. "I'm not sure what Aunt Mary would say about that," he said quietly.

Perry, who had been listening nearby, spoke up with a laugh. "I can't afford to pay you that much. But he's got a big farm, and it's a good opportunity."

John smiled and leaned in a little. "Why don't you come by tomorrow afternoon to take a look at the place? Me and my wife will be there. We can show you around."

Knox hesitated just a moment longer before nodding. "Okay... Thank you, sir."

With a firm handshake, John turned to Perry and asked, "How much do I owe you for the molasses?"

"Twenty-five cents, please," Perry replied.

John fished a quarter from his pocket, and Perry slid the jar across the counter.

"Thank you, John. Watch out for them horse thieves. I hear they got into Edward Hicks' barn a few nights ago," Perry said.

"I heard. Me and my friend Mr. Colt have been watching for them," John replied with a grin.

As he exited the store, he flashed a smile and called over his shoulder, "Talk to you tomorrow, young man," waving to Knox as he walked out.

Knox and Perry returned to their work, the soft murmur of their conversation blending with the winter stillness outside.

The Whittemeyer farm sprawled across the land, with fields stretching as far as the eye could see. A large barn stood behind a modest farmhouse, its weathered wood a quiet testament to many fruitful harvests. Chickens meandered across the yard, clucking as John Whittemeyer dropped feed, watching them eagerly rush to the scattered grains.

Knox approached the farmhouse, his boots crunching the frost-covered ground beneath him.

"Good day, Mr. Whittemeyer," Knox called out from a distance.

John looked up, dusting his hands on his trousers. "Knox, right?"

"Yes, sir."

John waved him over with a nod. "C'mon. I'll show you around."

Knox followed John as he scattered the rest of the feed across the yard, the chickens clucking excitedly around them. John led him to the far side of the property past a row of apple trees.

"We'll plant the corn here in March," John explained, gesturing to the sprawling, barren field. "Over yonder is the tobacco field."

As they walked, Emily Whittemeyer, a slender woman in her 40s with the quiet grace of a farmer's wife, approached them. She smiled warmly, extending a hand.

"Hello, I'm Emily."

Knox turned to her and offered a respectful smile. "I'm Knox. Pleased to meet you."

"Are you hungry?" she asked. "I just made lunch."

Before Knox could respond, a small toddler, no more than 18 months old, toddled over to Emily. Knox smiled, his expression softening as he waved at the child.

"This is Johnny," Emily introduced, lifting the boy into her arms.

Knox crouched down, meeting the little one at eye level. "He's a handsome little fella," he said with a warm smile.

John watched the interaction, a small smile crossing his face. "Do you want to see the cabin where you'll stay?"

Knox stood up, brushing off the dirt from his trousers. "Oh, yes sir," he replied eagerly.

John gestured toward a small cabin in the distance, a humble structure tucked away near the trees. As they walked toward it, Emily, holding Johnny in her arms, turned and headed back toward the main house.

♦ ♦ ♦ ♦ ♦ ♦

As dusk began to settle over the farm, Knox and John stood near the barn, the sky fading into a muted orange. The crisp air filled the space between them, and the quiet of the evening brought a sense of peace to the land.

"So, what do you think?" John asked, his hands resting on his hips as he studied Knox.

Knox took a slow glance around the farm, his eyes lingering on the vast fields and the simple yet sturdy buildings. His mind worked over the offer.

"Fifteen dollars a week?" Knox asked, making sure he had heard correctly.

"Yes, " John replied, nodding. "If you stay on for a year."

Knox nodded slowly, taking it in. "Like I said, you can stay in the cabin while you're here. "

Knox looked around again, his gaze softening as he surveyed the quiet farm. After a moment, he cracked a slight smile.

"I'll start next Sunday," Knox said, his voice steady. "Is it alright if I bring some of my things by Friday or Saturday?"

John smiled, extending his hand for a firm handshake. "Of course," he said, his voice chipper.

The two men shook hands as the evening darkened around them.

◆ ◆ ◆ ◆ ◆ ◆

Knox carried a chair through a small, dimly lit hut. The dirt floor was covered in dust, and the air was thick with the scent of incense. He stepped outside, placed the chair into a wagon, then came back inside.

"That's the last one," Knox said, his voice echoing slightly in the cramped space.

He walked over to Aunt Mary, a 70-year-old Jamaican woman, hunched over in a chair by the fire. Mary was peculiar and Knox wasn't sure what to make of her. He wasn't sure about her belief in voodoo, but he didn't discount it either. After all, he had seen enough in his life to know that some things weren't as simple as they seemed.

Knox kissed her forehead, the gesture soft and filled with the tenderness of long-standing affection.

Aunt Mary looked up, her expression full of concern. "So where is it you are moving to?"

Knox straightened, looking around the hut before answering. "Aunt Mary, I promise I won't be too far away. I found some work across Bell's Bend on the

Whittemeyer farm. It's right across the river. I'll still come see you when I can."

Aunt Mary shook her head slowly, her voice laced with doubt. "When you can? I don't know about this. I enjoy having you around. Mr. Perry is full of love and light. He's been so good to you. You ought to stay at his store."

Knox sighed, the frustration barely contained in his voice. "Mr. Whittemeyer is going to pay me fifteen dollars a week over at that farm! I ain't never made that much money! I can send some back home to momma and still have enough to live on. I… I have to go."

Aunt Mary's expression darkened. She leaned forward, her tone growing heavy. "I know how much you love your mother. But fifteen dollars is not what you think it is, my boy. Don't you know? Your soul is priceless! It just don't feel right. Not one bit! Mr. Whittemeyer is not a good man."

Knox looked at her with skepticism, an odd look crossing his face.

Aunt Mary's voice dropped lower, more urgent. "A year or two ago, I heard he hit one of his field hands working his tobacco crop. Broke his arm, and the man couldn't work for months…"

Knox shook his head. He didn't believe her. "Aunt Mary, it finally feels right for the first time in a long time. I always felt like I had a hex on me back in Alabama, but ever since I got to Nashville, things are really starting to get better."

Aunt Mary was silent for a long moment. Then, her gaze fixed on the fire, her humming and chanting filling the room as she entered a trance-like state. Her words came out slow and deliberate, as if they were being pulled from some unseen force.

"There is something evil on the farm! Knox, do you hear me?"

Knox's brow furrowed, but he nodded.

Aunt Mary's hands moved quickly, and she grabbed a vial of oil from the table. Still chanting softly, she poured the liquid into her palm and rubbed it onto Knox's forehead. Her touch was both firm and soothing.

"I won't tell you not to go," she said softly, her voice laden with warning. "But you must be careful around there! It's filled with darkness."

Knox nodded, his voice steady but laced with uncertainty. "Yes, ma'am. I will be careful."

◆ ◆ ◆ ◆ ◆ ◆

Knox sat on the edge of the bed in the small cabin, carefully unpacking his belongings from an old trunk. The cabin, though modest, had a quiet charm. The walls were simple, and the floor was rough, but it was a place to call his own. He worked in silence, the only sounds the rustling of clothes and the occasional creak of the floorboards.

As he finished, Emily entered, a warm smile on her face. She carried a bundle of freshly washed sheets and blankets, handing them to Knox.

"Here you are," she said kindly. "I don't want you to get cold. I just washed these."

Knox looked up at her, his face softening with gratitude. "Thank you, ma'am. I appreciate it."

Before Emily could respond, John appeared in the doorway, his voice carrying a quiet authority.

"Might want to get to bed," he said. "Tomorrow is

going to be a long day. There's a lot to do…"

Knox nodded, folding the blankets and tucking them neatly into the corner of the bed.

"Yes, sir," he replied respectfully.

Emily gave him one last warm look before she left the cabin, her footsteps fading as she returned to the house. Knox stood for a moment, staring at the simple dwelling that would be his home for the foreseeable future.

# Life on the Farm

The warmth of spring had begun to stretch across Middle Tennessee, coaxing the once-frozen soil to yield to the season of growth. It was a time of renewal, yet for Knox, it felt like the start of a long, unrelenting cycle. His body ached from the heavy labor, and each new day seemed to bring a new set of challenges.

◆ ◆ ◆ ◆ ◆ ◆

Knox led the horse out of the barn, its hooves clipping softly against the hard earth as they moved toward the field. The early morning light bathed everything in a soft, golden hue, and the coolness of the morning was still fresh on his skin. He was already feeling the weight of the day ahead as he moved quickly to attach the plow to the horse. The metal creaked as he worked, but his fingers were nimble as they secured the harness, his breath steady but strained.

Once the plow was attached, Knox clicked his tongue, urging the horse forward. The animal obeyed, walking steadily across the field, pulling the plow behind it. The sight should have been satisfying—a sign of progress—but Knox struggled to steer the plow. His hands gripped the reins tightly, sweat beading on his brow as the plow pulled unevenly through the soil. It was harder than it looked, and for every foot of progress he made, it felt like he was fighting against the land itself.

John Whittemeyer watched from the edge of the field, his arms crossed. He said nothing at first, merely observing Knox's struggle with a quiet intensity.

Knox finally managed to get the plow straight, but his back was already aching from the strain. As he worked, he noticed the long, barren stretch of land ahead of him. He would be out here for hours, trying to make the earth yield to his efforts.

After what felt like an eternity, Knox took a break to sow a row of seeds, bending down and gently placing them in the ground. His back throbbed with each motion, the familiar pain settling deep into his muscles. It felt as though his entire body was protesting, but he pressed on. As he worked, he noticed a row of seeds he had missed, a patch of bare earth where the crops should have been planted.

John approached, his boots crunching on the dirt. He pointed at the spot Knox had missed. "You missed one here," he said, his voice steady and matter-of-fact. Knox looked at the row and nodded. He reached down to correct the mistake, but his hands were shaking from fatigue.

As dusk fell over the farm, Knox was still at work. His back had stiffened from hours of bending and labor, but the work was far from done. He made his way to the pile of firewood, axe in hand, and began chopping. Each swing sent a sharp jolt through his body, and his movements were slower than they had been earlier in the day. The pain in his back was a constant reminder of just how much work lay ahead, but he couldn't stop. There was always more to do.

John Whittemeyer appeared in the doorway of the barn, his face shadowed by the fading light. He looked at Knox, his expression grim.

"Almost done, sir," Knox said, wiping the sweat from his brow with a handkerchief, though it was clear from the exhaustion in his voice that he was nowhere near finished.

"Have you fed the chickens yet?" John asked, his tone not harsh, but insistent.

Knox paused, his shoulders sagging as he turned toward John. "Sir, if it's okay, I'd like to go on back to the cabin. My back is really hurtin' me."

John's expression remained cold. "You know you have work to do. Best get to it."

Knox's heart sank. He wanted to argue, to tell John how hard the day had been, but the words wouldn't come. Instead, he just nodded and took up the axe again, his body screaming in protest. He couldn't stop now. Not when there was so much to be done.

John stood there for a moment, watching, before adding, "Don't forget to put some pepper in with the feed. It'll keep the squirrels away."

Knox sighed, the exhaustion taking over. "Yes, sir."

With slow, heavy steps, Knox walked back to the barn, the sound of his boots scraping on the dirt the only sound in the stillness of the evening. The farm stretched out before him, quiet and vast. The work was endless, but Knox needed the work. His momma needed the money. He would push through.

A few days later, the barn was quiet except for the soft rustle of hay and the occasional moo of the cows. Knox sat on a small stool beside one of the cows, his back hunched with the effort. The ache in his muscles was sharp, a constant reminder of the strain he had been under since he first arrived at the farm. He worked with a steady rhythm, milking the cow, but each movement sent a stab of pain through his back. His hands hurt, but he pushed through, focusing on the task at hand.

As Knox worked in the barn, he heard the soft sound of footsteps, and before he could turn, Emily appeared in the doorway, her figure framed by the fading light. A gentle smile touched her lips as she approached, a small basket in her hands.

"Here you are," she said, her voice warm and inviting, holding out a piece of bread and a jar of peach preserves. "I thought you might like something to eat. You've been working hard."

Knox looked up at her, a smile breaking across his face despite the persistent ache in his back. "Thank you, Miss Emily. That's kind of you." He took the bread and jar, feeling a small sense of relief wash over him at the break.

Emily nodded, her soft smile lingering as she turned to leave. "You're welcome," she said over her shoulder. Before she left, she paused and glanced back at him with a thoughtful expression. "Oh, I forgot to ask you—do you like cornbread? I was planning to make some tomorrow, and I was going to make an extra one for you to nibble on."

Knox's heart warmed at the thought of her kindness. "Oh, ma'am, I do love cornbread. But I had plans to go see Aunt Mary tomorrow when I get done with everything. Thank you." His words were sincere, and for a moment, he felt like life on the farm wasn't so bad.

Just then, little Johnny toddled into the barn, his small hands reaching up for Knox's leg. Without hesitation, the boy wrapped his arms around it, hugging him as best as his tiny arms could. Knox chuckled, reaching down to ruffle the boy's hair. "Hey there, little one," he said softly, smiling as Johnny giggled and let go.

Emily smiled at the tender moment, her eyes softening as she watched Knox interact with her son. She gave a small wave before turning to leave.

Knox returned to his sandwich, unwrapping the bread and taking a bite. The sweetness of the preserves mixed with the softness of the bread, offering him a brief moment of comfort in the midst of his exhaustion.

But just as he finished, John's stern voice broke through the quiet. He stood in the doorway of the barn, his brow wrinkled, a hint of frustration in his eyes.

"The cows need milking, Knox," John said, making it clear he wasn't pleased with the delay.

Caught off guard, Knox straightened up, wincing slightly at the sharp pain in his back. His face flushed, and he looked almost sheepish. "Yes, sir," he muttered, turning back to the cow.

Knox hesitated, his voice unsure as he looked up at John. "Um, sir," he began, "When are you going to pay me for last week?"

John remained silent for a moment, then begrudgingly reached into his pocket and pulled out ten banknotes. He counted them quickly before handing them to Knox.

His movements were slow, as if the task was beneath him, but he didn't speak a word. He simply nodded toward the cows.

"Finish the milking," John said curtly, his tone colder than before. Then, without another glance, he turned and walked out of the barn.

Knox stood there for a moment, holding the money

in his hands, staring at it as his frustration grew. He quickly counted the bills again—still only ten dollars. His blood began to boil as he realized he was being shorted.

"John! Sir!" Knox called out, but by the time the words left his mouth, John had already disappeared into the house. The door shut behind him with a finality that made Knox grit his teeth in frustration.

"Damn it," he muttered under his breath, his anger rising as he shoved the bread aside. He quickly finished his sandwich, then plopped back down onto the stool. His back screamed in protest with every movement, but he had to finish.

As he resumed milking the cow, he reached back to rub his sore lower back. The relief was fleeting. Each movement sent fresh waves of pain through his body, and he couldn't help but grimace.

The backbreaking labor, and the unfairness of his pay gnawed at him, but there was nothing he could do about it.

◆ ◆ ◆ ◆ ◆ ◆

The flames in the Aunt Mary's fireplace flickered, followed by the occasional popping and snapping of the burning wood. The air was thick with the scent of herbs and smoke. Knox sat on a worn-out chair, his posture stiff, as Aunt Mary sat opposite him. Her face, aged and weathered by time, was etched with concern. Her gaze pierced through him, as if she could see the very thoughts swirling in his mind.

"Tell me," Aunt Mary spoke, her voice steady yet laced with worry. "Are they treating you right on the farm?"

Knox shifted in his seat, the tension in his shoulders evident. A flicker of hesitation crossed his face before he answered, the words feeling heavy on his tongue.

"Miss Emily is really nice. She makes the best preserves. They're better than momma's. She brings me food sometimes," he said, his voice soft, as though the warmth of Emily's kindness was the only comfort in the cold, unyielding world of the farm.

"And the man of the house?" Aunt Mary asked, her eyes narrowing slightly as if she already knew the answer.

Knox hesitated again, the memories of Mr. Whittemeyer's stern, calculating demeanor flooding his mind. He took a deep breath before answering, his voice tight.

"He can be quite stern. Seems like he's always watching over me."

Aunt Mary's eyes flashed with a fierce intensity. "I told you! His heart is evil."

Knox's unease deepened, his gut tightening as Aunt Mary's words hung heavy in the air. He looked away, as if trying to dismiss the warning, but her words struck a chord.

"He didn't pay me all my wages last week," Knox said after a long pause, his voice quieter now, almost reluctant to speak the truth. "He still owes me five dollars."

Aunt Mary's eyes darkened, a scowl etched into her face. Her hand trembled as she reached toward the flames. Her voice, when it came, was filled with sharp clarity.

"That's the darkness in him! I've been trying to tell

you!" she exclaimed, her voice rising with urgency. "Your momma needs that money!"

She shuffled toward the fireplace, her movements deliberate and swift despite her age. Knox watched her, feeling a rising knot of fear in his stomach.

"Look into the fire with me!" Aunt Mary's voice was commanding now, filled with authority.

Knox scooted forward in his chair, drawn into her gaze. The crackling fire cast strange shapes on the walls, and for a moment, he swore he saw a hand reach out of the flames. Aunt Mary seemed to go into a trance, her murmurs growing softer, rhythmic, as if she were communing with something beyond this world.

Suddenly, her voice cut through the silence.

"No! No!" Aunt Mary's outburst startled Knox, and his heart raced in his chest. Her eyes were wide now, her eyes fixed on something unseen in the flickering shadows.

"Go over there and collect your money," she said, her voice trembling but forceful. "It's late. His soul is tired."

Knox's heart hammered in his chest as the knot of fear tightened further. He didn't want to go, didn't want to face Mr. Whittemeyer, but Aunt Mary's voice was insistent. Her eyes, full of intensity, locked onto his.

"I must warn you," she continued, her voice laden with dread, "You have to use extreme caution. He is very dangerous!"

The crackling of the log in the fireplace filled the room as the tension between them grew. Knox's mind raced. Was she right? Could there be something truly dark within Mr. Whittemeyer? The doubt gnawed at him, but the fear was stronger now, pressing down on his chest.

"He sees the light in you. He wants it for himself!" Aunt Mary's voice was nearly a hiss now, and Knox's breath caught in his throat.

He was torn—conflicted between his fear and his growing sense of duty. Aunt Mary raised her voice once more, louder, desperate.

"My boy, he ain't gonna pay you. His soul is black!"

Knox fidgeted in his seat, unable to sit still. Aunt Mary's words were sinking deeper into his mind, turning his insides into a churning mess. He didn't know what to think, what to believe.

Aunt Mary's voice rose again, fierce and commanding. "He's going to try to take your life!"

Her eyes blazed with an intensity that almost seemed otherworldly, and Knox's fear intensified as she locked eyes with him.

"Stand up! Give me your handkerchief!" Aunt Mary demanded, her tone no longer soft or patient, but sharp, filled with authority.

Knox's hand trembled as he reached into his pocket and pulled out his handkerchief. He handed it to her, his chest tightening. She hobbled over to a shrine in the corner of the room, picking up a small trinket from a shelf. She placed it carefully inside the handkerchief and tied it up tightly.

"Get me that pitcher," Aunt Mary commanded, pointing to a pitcher on a shelf across the room. Knox, almost in a daze, fetched it and held onto it for dear life.

Aunt Mary picked up a pot near the fire and placed the handkerchief inside, muttering something under her breath. "Pour the water over it," she instructed.

Knox didn't understand, but he followed her command, his confusion growing. As the water boiled, Aunt Mary pulled out herbs from a jar and sprinkled them into the pot, her chants growing louder. The room seemed to thicken with tension, the fire crackling as if it had a life of its own.

"What are you..." Knox began, but Aunt Mary interrupted him, her voice firm.

"Hush!"

The water began to bubble, and Aunt Mary used a poker to fish out the handkerchief. She placed it carefully on the hearth, untied it, and retrieved the trinket. She wrapped some twine around it and made it into a necklace.

"This gris-gris will protect you. Don't ever take it off!" Aunt Mary said firmly, placing the necklace around Knox's neck.

Knox looked at her, his chest tight with fear and uncertainty. He wanted to argue, wanted to question her, but the fierce intensity in her eyes stopped him.

"Now go! Go get the money that he owes you!" Aunt Mary urged, her voice rising with impatience.

Knox's heart pounded in his chest, his body torn between fear and obedience. He didn't want to go. The darkness of the night, Aunt Mary's words, and the uncertainty of what awaited him paralyzed him for a moment.

Aunt Mary leaned in, her face inches from his. Her eyes burned with an intensity that seemed to pierce right through him. "You are protected, my boy! Go!"

Without another word, Knox stormed out of the hut, slamming the door behind him. The night air hit his face like a slap, but it did nothing to clear his mind. His heart raced as he hesitated for a moment, staring at the hut behind him. Through the window, he could see Aunt Mary still chanting, her figure silhouetted in the glow of the fire.

Knox took a deep breath, his mind clouded with fear, uncertainty, and a strange sense of destiny. He turned and headed toward the Whittemeyer farmhouse.

# The Broken Spoke

The crackling of the fire in the hearth echoed through the farmhouse, mingling with the cries of the Whittemeyers' 18-month-old son. The baby's wails filled the air, adding to the exhaustion and frustration that had been building in the room. John and Emily were sitting by the fire, their faces drawn with fatigue.

Filled with concern, Emily broke the silence. "Why can't we just put him in bed with us?" she asked softly yet tinged with desperation.

Tired and irritated, John Whittemeyer rubbed his temples before responding. "Honey, if we keep bringing him into our bed, he's never going to sleep in his crib."

Emily, her eyes filled with pain as she listened to their son cry, glanced toward the door, a sense of helplessness in her expression. "It just pains me to hear him cry. He can sleep with me on my side," she suggested, reaching her arms out as if to comfort the child.

Before John could respond, an urgent knock at the door interrupted them. Annoyed, John stood up abruptly and threw on a robe as he strode toward the door, muttering under his breath.

"Who is it?" John barked, the irritation in his voice clear.

"It's Knox, sir," came the muffled response, his voice tight with barely-contained frustration.

He swung the door open, and there stood Knox, his face etched with urgency.

Knox stepped inside, his eyes burning with determination.

John Whittemeyer's patience wore thin, his temper flared at the unexpected visitor. "What do you need? Don't you realize what time it is?"

Knox didn't waste any time. "You didn't pay me all my money!"

John's expression shifted from annoyance to disbelief, his anger rising. "It's getting late," he said, glancing back at Emily, who was sitting silently, her concern growing. "I'm trying to settle my son. Can this not wait?"

Knox's resolve hardened. He stepped closer, his voice growing more insistent with each word. "No, sir. Why won't you pay me what you owe?"

John's anger flared. He strode toward the door, grabbed Knox by the shoulder, and shoved him roughly out of the house. "Get out!" he demanded, his voice rising with fury as he slammed the door behind him.

Enraged, Knox's eyes darted around, and his gaze landed on a wagon wheel lying on the porch. His breath came in ragged gasps, and a primitive, guttural growl escaped his throat. His hands clenched into fists, and with a violent kick, he shattered the wheel into several pieces. The sound of it breaking seemed to fuel his rage, and through the door, he could hear John's cursing him, which only served to fan the flames of his anger.

Knox's heart pounded in his chest, the raw emotion threatening to tear him apart. He reached down and picked up one of the broken pieces of the wagon spoke. His knuckles turned white as he gripped it tightly, the tension building in his muscles. He was seething now, barely able to hold himself back.

Without thinking, he pushed the door open again, stepping into the home. Before he could say a word, John rushed toward him, shoving him hard. Knox barely budged, his body feeling like a stone against the force. Knox wasn't going to back down.

His frustration boiled over. With a sudden surge of strength, he pushed back with a strength that surprised John. The impact sent John stumbling, his anger faltering for a moment.

Without warning, Knox swung the wagon spoke with deadly force. The sickening thud as it struck John's face rang out in the quiet house. Emily gasped in horror, her hands flying to her mouth, but the damage had been done. John crumpled to the ground, blood trickling from his right eyebrow.

"Pay me what you owe!" Knox shouted, his voice rough with rage.

A scuffle ensued. John, now barely conscious, pushed himself up, blood staining his face. "I said get out!" he growled, his voice weak but still full of fury.

Knox swung the spoke again, his movements fast and forceful. The impact was brutal, connecting with John's face once more, and the farmer crumpled to the floor in a bloody heap. Emily stood frozen in shock, her eyes wide as the violence unfolded before her.

"Pay me the money!" Knox demanded again, his voice trembling with fury.

Knox's actions were swift, desperate, and filled with an urgency that scared even him. He continued to strike John's limp body with the wagon spoke as the baby cried louder, its screams echoing through the house.

"Knox! Stop!" Emily cried out, her voice trembling with fear.

Emily placed Johnny on the bed and rushed toward Knox. In a panicked blur, she dug her fingernails into his face, trying to pull him away. With a swift push, Knox knocked her aside, the force of it sending her stumbling backward.

In his panic, Knox raised the wagon spoke again, and in a split second, it struck Emily's face. The blow was swift and brutal, and she collapsed to the ground, her body going limp as she hit the floor.

Knox froze, horror filling his chest. He stood there, trembling, as he looked at Emily, blood dripping from her cheek. Knox's breath hitched in his throat.

"Oh, Miss Emily!" he whispered. His hands trembled as he kneeled beside her.

"Ma'am, I'm so sorry…" Knox's voice broke as he placed his hand on her shoulder, but it did little to erase the guilt burning inside him.

With shaky hands, he discarded the broken wagon spoke, tossing it into the flames of the hearth. The fire crackled loudly, the heat rising as if to cleanse the violence from the room.

Knox turned toward the crying toddler, the sound now echoing painfully in his ears. He walked over to the crib, scooped the child into his arms, and rocked him gently.

"Shhh… It's ok, little Johnny," he whispered, trying to calm the baby's cries.

After a long moment, Knox turned back to Emily's limp body, his heart heavy with regret. He picked her up, placing her carefully on the bed. The baby, still crying, was placed on top of her mother. The crying gradually stopped.

"There you go," Knox said softly, his voice trembling.

He turned back to John's body, still lying

motionless on the floor. He walked over and, with a strained breath, picked up John's body, placing it next to Emily in the bed.

"Johnny," Knox whispered, addressing the child who was now peacefully resting between his parents, "You can lay next to your daddy if you want."

Knox turned toward the dresser, his eyes scanning the room. His hand hesitated before he picked up a wallet and some coins lying next to it. He also grabbed a black overcoat and walked back to where Johnny lay next to his parents.

"Goodnight, little one," Knox murmured, tucking Johnny in with a quilt.

He lingered for a moment, his heart torn. He glanced back at the small family, but the guilt of his actions weighed heavily. He had to get out of there.

With a final look at the peaceful baby, Knox turned and walked toward the door.

♦ ♦ ♦ ♦ ♦ ♦

Knox raced down a hill behind the farm, his breath ragged as his boots pounded against the ground. He reached a small clearing where a small dwelling sat near the edge of the water. His heart hammered in his chest, and though he tried to remain calm, the urgency of the situation consumed him.

He banged on the door, his fist striking the wood with a force that echoed through the night. No answer. He banged again frantically. After a few moments, the door creaked open, and Abe Hewland, a grizzled older ferry operator, peered out from behind it.

"I need to get across, sir," Knox said, his voice tight

with tension.

Abe looked him over, taking in Knox's disheveled state, the wild look in his eyes. "Son, it's gettin' late," Abe said, his voice rough but not unkind. "Won't you just come back in the mornin'?"

Knox's hands fumbled into his pockets. He pulled out five banknotes. Without even glancing at them, he thrust the money into Abe's hand. The ferryman's eyes widened as he saw the large sum.

"Alright, son," Abe said, his tone shifting as he took the money. "Come with me."

Without another word, the two of them made their way to the ferry. The boat creaked beneath their weight as they boarded. Abe moved to the front of the boat, picking up the oars with practiced ease.

With his mind still racing, Knox walked to the other end of the boat, needing the space, needing silence. There was no need for conversation. He barely acknowledged Abe as the ferryman spoke, his voice carrying softly in the stillness of the night.

"The full moon looks pretty on the water tonight," Abe said, his eyes scanning the reflection on the surface.

But Knox didn't respond. His gaze was fixed on the distant shore, the urgency in his chest growing with every passing second.

The full moon cast its eerie glow across the river, the water shimmering as it flowed beneath the silent night. The ferryman rowed slowly, the rhythmic sound of the oars breaking the otherwise still air. On the small boat, Knox paced back and forth, his steps restless, his body a coiled spring. The reflection of the moon danced across the water, but the peaceful scene did little to calm his mind. Each dip of the oars into the river seemed to echo the rhythm of his own racing heart.

As the ferry slowly moved across the river, the shore began to fade into the distance. But the peace of the river did nothing to calm the storm inside him. Knox's thoughts whirled, his mind a blur of regret and fear. What had he done? And where was he even going to go now?

◆ ◆ ◆ ◆ ◆ ◆

Aunt Mary's cabin was dimly lit, the crackling fire casting ominous figures on the walls. Knox stepped inside, the door creaking behind him as he entered. The air was thick with the scent of incense and herbs, and in the corner of the room, Aunt Mary sat, her gaze fixed intently on the fire. The light from the flames illuminated her face, and for a moment, she appeared almost otherworldly, her eyes reflecting a deep, ancient wisdom.

Without looking up, Aunt Mary's voice cut through the silence, steady and commanding. "Take off that jacket. Throw it in the fire!"

Knox hesitated for only a second before pulling the jacket off and tossing it into the flames. The fire hissed violently as the fabric caught, and the room was momentarily engulfed in thick, black smoke. Knox coughed, his eyes stinging. Aunt Mary sat unmoved, as though the smoke didn't affect her at all.

As the smoke began to clear, Aunt Mary finally raised her eyes to meet his, her face softening. "Oh, look at your nose. It's just a little scratch," she said, her voice soft but firm. "I told you you'd be protected."

Knox squirmed as she stared at him. He could feel her eyes on him, watching him, seeing through him. The anxiety tightened in his chest, a knot he couldn't shake.

"He didn't want to pay me," Knox muttered, his voice barely above a whisper, the shame of what he had done washed all over him.

Aunt Mary's eyes narrowed, studying him closely, her sharp gaze never leaving his face. "I no longer sense the darkness," she said, her voice soft, but filled with knowing. "Did you..."

Knox's silence was the loudest answer. He couldn't bring himself to speak of what had transpired, the guilt flooding him like a tidal wave. His silence spoke volumes.

Aunt Mary's voice broke through the quiet, this time tinged with something else — something softer, almost approving. "I asked the lwa to deliver you, and they did."

A sense of awe washed over Knox, mingling with the gnawing guilt that clawed at his conscience. He sank into a chair across from Aunt Mary, his hands shaking uncontrollably as he struggled to process what had happened, what he had become. The truth of his actions was undeniable, and the weight of it suffocated him.

Aunt Mary's voice was softer now but still carried an air of unshakable certainty. "You have found favor with Bondye."

Her words, meant to offer comfort, fell on Knox's ears like cold stone. There was no warmth, no solace in them, only a reminder of the price he had paid. He closed his eyes, his mind reeling, unsure of where to go from here, of what it all meant.

"What should I do?" Knox asked, his voice barely above a whisper.

Aunt Mary's lips curled into a wicked grin, her

eyes gleaming with an almost supernatural knowing. She paused for a moment, letting the silence stretch between them, before she spoke again.

"Stay away from the Whittemeyer farm," Aunt Mary advised, her voice sharp, as if the words themselves carried a warning. "That place is cursed now. You've got no business there."

Knox shifted uneasily, his mind racing with the possibilities. "I can't go downtown either," he muttered, staring at the floor. "But maybe I should start walking toward Clarksville. Catch a steamboat west. Ride to St. Louis, then take a train to Kansas or Oklahoma. No one will be looking for me there."

Aunt Mary's gaze hardened as she scolded him. "No! There'll be people at the docks and train stations waiting for you. They know you'll try to flee."

She paused for a moment, her eyes narrowing as if considering her next words carefully. "Go see Mr. Berry at the stables. He might have a horse you can use. Get on back home to Alabama."

Knox stared at her, the weight of her words pressing down on him. His heart pounded in his chest, and the thought of being discovered made his palms sweat. "I don't want to go into town," he said, his voice tight with anxiety. "People will see me. I can't risk it."

Aunt Mary's expression darkened, her smile fading into a more serious look. She reached out, placing a hand on Knox's arm, her touch surprisingly firm. "Honey, Bondye is watching over you, but you gotta get back home before things get worse. If you stay here, they're gonna hang you!"

Her words were blunt, but they carried a chilling truth.

Knox nodded slowly. There was no escaping what he did, no way to outrun the consequences. But maybe there was a way out of Nashville — out of the grip of the law.

"Alright," he muttered, more to himself than to her. "I'll go see Mr. Berry."

Aunt Mary's smile returned, but it was no longer wicked — it was knowing, as if she had already seen his path unfold before him. "Good boy," she said softly. "Now go. Time's runnin' out."

Knox stood up, his body still aching, but his resolve solidified. He turned toward the door, his mind set on the next step. Aunt Mary's firm voice stopped him. She pointed at the gris-gris around his neck. "Don't you ever take it off!" she commanded.

"Yes ma'am," he replied, his hand instinctively rubbing the handmade necklace as he stepped toward the door.

# On the Run

The pale light of the morning sun stretched across the Whittemeyer farm as Patton Foster, a well-dressed man in his 30s, approached the farmhouse. He knocked on the door, but there was no response. The sound of a baby's cries echoed from inside, sharp and frantic, growing more insistent with each passing moment.

"Anybody home?" Patton called out firmly but laced with concern. He knocked again, a little louder this time.

"Emily? John?" he said, waiting for any sign of life within the cabin.

Hearing no answer, he tried the door handle. It was unlocked. Patton pushed the door open.

"Sister, is it okay if I come in?"

Patton entered quietly, his eyes scanning the room. The baby's cries were louder now, more desperate. His eyes landed on Emily and John, lying motionless in the bed. The room was heavy with silence, interrupted only by the baby's screams. The scene before him was one of horror. John and Emily both lay in bed, their bodies eerily still atop crimson stained sheets. Their infant son, Johnny, crawled aimlessly on top of his mother's body, oblivious to the tragedy that surrounded him.

Patton moved closer, his eyes narrowing in disbelief. He froze as he tried to process what he was seeing.

"John!" Patton's voice cracked as he reached for his brother-in-law. With a quick motion, he rolled John onto his back. The sight of John's face caused his stomach to drop. The right side of his face had been caved in. Patton couldn't speak, his breath catching in his throat. He was too stunned to cry, the sight almost too much to bear.

"Come here, Johnny," Patton said softly, his voice now a protective whisper as he carefully picked up his nephew from the bed. He shielded the child's eyes from the scene before him, his arms tightening around him as he cradled the little boy close.

Patton took a deep, shaky breath, his mind reeling. He walked around the bed and gently rolled Emily over. The horror on her face was even worse — her features were unrecognizable, her face a bloody mess. A wave of grief hit him hard, tears welling in his eyes as he looked down at her lifeless form.

He stood there for a moment, unable to process the overwhelming reality of it all. His nephew's cries were the only sound in the cabin, and they cut through the silence like a knife.

"It's okay. You're okay," Patton whispered softly, his voice shaky but steady. He rocked Johnny gently in his arms, trying to comfort the child, even as his own world felt like it was falling apart.

"Uncle Patton's got you," he whispered to the baby, holding him close. His gaze fell on John and Emily, the grief and shock so overwhelming that it left him breathless.

Patton stepped out of the cabin, the door creaking softly behind him as he closed it. He stood for a moment on the porch, the weight of the world pressing down on him. The sky was clear, the sun bright, but everything felt dimmed by the horror inside.

His heart was broken, his thoughts scattered, but he knew what he had to do next. He had to keep his nephew safe and alert authorities.

♦ ♦ ♦ ♦ ♦ ♦

The afternoon sun hung high in the sky over the Whittemeyer cabin. Sheriff John Price, a hard-nosed lawman in his 50s with no sense of humor, stood on the porch with Jim Norris, a long-time deputy whose demeanor was much friendlier than one would expect from law enforcement.

Sheriff Price's voice was firm as he spoke, giving his orders with the precision of someone used to authority.

"Coroner Peebles should be here in a few hours. Keep the place secure. Don't let anyone in there," he commanded.

Deputy Norris nodded respectfully. "Yes, sir."

Without another word, Sheriff Price mounted his horse-drawn wagon, flicked the reins, and rode off, leaving Norris standing in the midday heat.

Deputy Norris watched for a moment before turning and heading toward the porch. He sat down heavily on the step. It was going to be a long day.

A man on horseback approached the cabin, his figure silhouetted against the afternoon sky. Deputy Norris stood up immediately.

"Halt!" he called as he stepped forward.

The rider pulled his horse to a stop with a soft grunt. He was a young man in his 20s, wearing a nice hat and a crisp suit jacket, giving off the air of a young professional.

"Good afternoon, Deputy," the man greeted, his voice friendly and eager as he dismounted with a fluid motion. "I'm Scott Singer from the *Tennessean*."

He extended his hand with a wide, friendly grin.

Deputy Norris hesitated for a moment before shaking it, his grip firmly.

"I'm sorry, sir," Deputy Norris said, his voice polite but firm. "Reporters aren't allowed in the house. The coroner should be here pretty soon to conduct an investigation."

Singer's eyes flickered with curiosity, his smile undeterred. "Can you tell me what happened?" he asked. "I was in the area investigating the band of horse thieves that've been hitting local farms. A fella over at Lucky's Tavern mentioned the Whittemeyers were murdered last night."

Deputy Norris sighed, his eyes drifting toward the cabin as he considered his words carefully. "We don't know much," he said. "Mrs. Whittemeyer's brother found 'em. We can't find Mr. Whittemeyer's wallet. It was probably a robbery, but there might be more to it. Whoever did it had a vendetta. Mr. Whittemeyer was beaten so badly that his right eye rolled out of his socket when we tried to move him."

Singer winced, the grim detail clearly taking him off guard. "Oh my," he muttered under his breath, his expression momentarily turning to one of shock.

"Do you have any leads?" he asked, his curiosity now piqued, his reporter instincts kicking in. Deputy Norris nodded, his expression hardening as he thought over the details. "Well, the ferry operator down the street told me a guy named Knox Martin had been working for the family for a month or two. Last night, he paid to take the ferry back across the river around ten o'clock."

Norris paused for a moment, as if collecting his thoughts. "The man who runs the ferry was pretty adamant that Knox was wearing a black coat that belonged to Mr. Whittemeyer. We'll probably have an arrest warrant by the end of the day. We're just waiting for the coroner to file his report."

Scott Singer's eyes widened slightly. "So, you think Knox Martin is the man who killed them?"

Deputy Norris nodded. "We don't know for sure, but the evidence points that way. He was one of the last people to see Mr. Whittemeyer alive, and if he took his coat, that's a pretty damning piece of evidence."

Singer's pen moved along a notepad as he jotted down the details. "I appreciate the information, deputy" he said as he nodded toward Norris.

Deputy Norris gave him a short nod, his thoughts clearly elsewhere as he glanced toward the cabin.

◆ ◆ ◆ ◆ ◆ ◆

Knox walked cautiously through the alleys of downtown Nashville, keeping his head down to avoid being seen. His footsteps were quick but deliberate, each movement calculated to avoid attention. He could feel the eyes of the city watching, even though he was hidden in the shadows.

He finally slipped into a livery stable, the scent of hay and leather filling the air. Knox paused, scanning the space. He saw a young man tending to a horse, his back turned. With a deep breath, Knox approached cautiously.

"Where's George?" Knox asked.

The young man looked up briefly, his eyes lingering on Knox before nodding toward the back. "He's over at Red's Tavern."

Knox nodded in thanks, then turned and strode out of the stable, his mind already focused on the next step.

He had no time to waste.

Looking over his shoulder, Knox slipped around the corner into a small tavern on Cherry Street, his nerves obvious in the stiffness of his movements. The moment he entered, a few heads turned his way, and the soft murmur of conversation stopped. His heart raced as he scanned the room, trying to stay calm despite their uneasy stares. He made his way to the bar, trying to act natural as he approached George Berry, a 40-year-old African American man who waved him over.

"Knox, is that you?" George asked, his voice friendly and welcoming. He motioned for him to come closer.

Knox hesitated for just a second before moving toward George. "Yeah, it's me. Good to see you, sir."

As he approached, several patrons in the tavern noticed him and began whispering amongst themselves. Knox felt their eyes following him, and he shifted uncomfortably.

"Is it true, Knox?" George asked, his voice softer now, carrying a note of concern.

Knox tensed. He wasn't sure how to respond. "Not sure what you mean," he replied, his voice strained. He tried to play it off like he had no idea what George was talking about, but the nerves were starting to get to him.

George raised an eyebrow and reached over the bar, pulling out a newspaper. He slapped it down in front of Knox.

The headline read: **"KNOX MARTIN WANTED FOR BELL'S BEND MURDERS."**

Knox's heart sank as he stared at the paper. His stomach twisted in knots.

Just then, one of the men in the bar who had been

staring at Knox suddenly rushed out the door. Knox's nerves kicked into overdrive. He could feel his anxiety rising. He didn't belong here—not anymore.

Sensing his discomfort, George leaned in slightly. "Calm down, Knox," he said in a low voice. "What do you need, son?"

Just then, two police officers rushed into the tavern. Instinctively, Knox jumped over the bar and darted out the back door.

Knox ran through the streets of Nashville, the pulse of his heart pounding in his ears, his breath coming in short gasps. As he darted past horse-drawn carriages and bustling pedestrians, Knox barely noticed them. His only focus was the escape, the blur of downtown Nashville barely registering in his mind.

Every step was a frantic push forward, his legs burning as they carried him further down the narrow street. He could hear the rhythmic pounding of his feet against the cobblestones, a sound that seemed far too loud in the chaos of the chase. The police officers behind him shouted orders but Knox didn't dare look back. His only thought was escape, the fear of capture propelling him faster, his legs feeling as if they might give out any moment.

He had to keep moving. He couldn't be caught.

Knox shot a glance over his shoulder, just for a second, just enough to see the officers gaining ground on him. But that moment of distraction proved costly. Without warning, he slammed into a horse-drawn wagon that had been crossing the street, the sudden impact knocking him off his feet. The jolt sent shockwaves through his body as he hit the ground hard, pain flaring through his side.

Before he could scramble to his feet, the officers were on him. Hands grabbed at his arms, pulling him roughly to the cobblestones. His heart pounded in his chest, the sting of panic rising as he struggled. The officers worked swiftly, tying his hands with rope, the rough fibers cutting into his skin.

"You're under arrest," one of the officers said, his voice cold and final.

Knox's heart sank. Reality slammed into him like the cart he'd collided with. His fight had come to an end, and there was no way out this time. He could only stare at the cobblestones beneath him, the sound of the street bustling on as though nothing had changed. But everything had changed.

A rough hand yanked him to his feet, and the officers shoved him forward. He barely registered the onlookers who had gathered, some looking in confusion, others with disapproving glares, but none of it mattered.

The officers walked him through the streets, his wrists bound, and the crowd seemed to part before them, the eyes of the city on him as they made their way toward the jail wagon waiting further down the street. The sound of the crowd's whispers echoed in his ears, but Knox kept his gaze forward. There was no way out of this.

# An Angry Mob

Officer Michael Prater led Knox down a narrow corridor of the jail, the echo of their footsteps ringing off the stone walls. At the end of the hallway, Jailer Adam Graves, a 50-year-old overweight man with a pencil pusher's demeanor, looked up from his desk, glancing at the two as they approached.

Jailer Graves didn't waste any time and immediately pulled out a piece of paper to take notes.

"Who you got here?" Graves asked flatly.

"Knox Martin," Officer Prater answered flatly. "He's the man wanted for the murder over in Bell's Bend."

Graves looked Knox over briefly before nodding and continuing to write. Officer Prater led Knox to a small holding cell. Defeated, Knox stepped inside and took a seat. The cell door slammed shut, and he lowered his head.

◆ ◆ ◆ ◆ ◆ ◆

Later that evening, William Thompson, a tall, balding police detective in his 40s, walked down the narrow hall of the small jail. As he passed the cells, the prisoners on both sides fell silent. Thompson's presence commanded respect as he approached the cell where Knox was being held.

"Can you let me in?" Thompson asked.

He motioned for Jailer Graves to get up and let him into Knox's cell. Graves waddled over, unlocked the cell, and quickly closed the door behind him as he entered.

Thompson stood in front of Knox, his posture rigid. He looked up, his body jumpy from the anxiety, his eyes darting around, unable to focus on one thing for too long.

"Knox Martin?" Thompson asked, his tone stern, but with an underlying sense of patience.

Knox nodded, his voice trembling as he answered, "Yes, sir."

"Can I get you a cup of water?" Thompson offered, his voice softer now, attempting to ease the tension.

Knox shook his head, his hands wringing together nervously. "No, sir."

"Would you like some coffee?" Thompson asked, his voice still calm.

Again, Knox shook his head.

"Son, you know why you're here, don't you?" Thompson's voice became more serious.

Knox nodded quickly, avoiding Thompson's eyes. He couldn't speak, the guilt and fear choking him.

"Look," Thompson continued, his tone softening slightly, "The ferry operator has been telling us all about what you did on the night of the murder."

Knox's body stiffened, but he remained silent.

"He also says that you took something that belonged to Mr. Whittemeyer. Is that true? Did you rob the Whittemeyers?".

Knox shifted uneasily, still refusing to speak. He couldn't bear to explain himself.

"I need you to tell me what happened," Thompson continued, his voice growing more insistent. "Why were you in their house on the night of the murder? Did you go there to kill Mr. Whittemeyer and his wife?"

Knox took a deep breath, his eyes squeezing shut

for a moment. His voice cracked as he spoke, his words barely a whisper.

"I didn't want to kill them, especially Miss Emily," he admitted, the sob catching in his throat.

Thompson's demeanor softened as he watched Knox. "What happened? Why'd you do it?"

Before Knox could answer, Sheriff Price appeared in the background, standing just outside the bars, watching the exchange with quiet intensity.

"I went to the house to see if Mr. Whittemeyer was going to pay me the money he owed me," Knox began, his voice breaking. "We got into an argument, and he shoved me. Aunt Mary told me he was going to kill me. I had to do it. I had nothing against his wife. She grabbed ahold of me, and I hit her.

Knox rubbed his eyes, trying to remain composed.

"I beat them with a wagon spoke. Once I was done, I threw it in the fire."

Tears filled Knox's eyes. The burden of his confession was too much, and the grief over what he'd done finally broke through.

Thompson looked at him for a long moment, his face serious. "Who is Aunt Mary?" he asked, his voice filled with disbelief.

Knox wiped his eyes with the back of his hand, his voice trembling. "She's a voodoo lady, sir. She is mighty old, but she's a powerful woman."

Thompson stared at him, unable to comprehend the story Knox was telling, the absurdity of it mixing with the horror of his confession.

"I didn't touch the child, I swear," Knox added quickly. "I pulled the covers up so he wouldn't get cold. Is little Johnny okay?"

Thompson paused for a moment, his face softening just a fraction. "I think the boy's uncle is caring for him right now. I don't necessarily have all the details."

Knox began to sob, his body shaking.

"What's gonna happen to me?" he asked through his tears, his voice cracking.

Thompson sighed, his face growing serious once again. "You are being charged with murder. It's not really up to me what happens. A jury of your peers will decide all that."

"They gonna hang me, ain't they?" Knox asked, his voice filled with raw fear.

Thompson paused, his eyes meeting Knox's for a long moment. "I don't know, son."

Knox's sobs grew louder as he fell into a pit of hopelessness. Thompson stood to leave, placing a hand on Knox's shoulder in a rare moment of empathy.

"You did the right thing by confessing," Thompson said softly. "I'll see to it that they treat you right while you're in here."

Still an emotional wreck, Knox wiped his eyes and nodded, grateful for the detective's kindness.

"Thank you, sir," Knox whispered.

Thompson motioned for Jailer Graves to open the cell.

As Graves unlocked the door, a strange noise suddenly echoed from outside the jail, causing Knox to freeze. A sense of unease crept over him, and he approached the door of his cell, pressing his ear between the cold bars to try to make sense of the sound.

"Sir, will you please let Aunt Mary know I'm okay?" Knox asked, his voice laced with quiet desperation.

Detective Thompson gave him a sympathetic glance. "Sure, son," he replied softly.

As Thompson approached Sheriff Price, who was scanning the streets outside through a window, the strange noise grew louder. It was unsettling, something that felt out of place, like a distant rumble growing closer. Thompson looked over at Price, his brow furrowed.

"What is that?" Thompson asked, his voice tense.

Price's eyes narrowed as he studied the growing disturbance outside. Alarm flashed across his face as he pulled his pistol from its holster.

"Damnit," Price muttered under his breath. "There's about forty of 'em headed this way. They're armed. I bet they want the prisoner."

Jailer Graves waddled over, nervously looking out the window as well. The crowd's noise was getting louder by the second. Graves began to visibly panic. Price turned away from the window, his face grim as he ran toward another window to get a better view.

"We're surrounded," he said, his voice heavy with tension.

"What do you want to do?" Thompson asked, his tone serious but calm.

Price's mind raced with urgency as he formulated a plan. He had little time, but he couldn't let them take his prisoner.

"I've got an idea," he said.

Price hurried to Knox's cell, his heart pounding as the mob got closer. He stopped in front of the bars and quickly gave his orders.

"Take off your clothes. Give them to the detective," Price said, his voice sharp. "Grab that blanket, too." He pointed at the bed.

Still reeling from everything that had happened, Knox hesitated only for a moment before complying, his hands shaking as he undressed.

Price turned to Thompson, who was standing nearby. "Give him your clothes," he instructed.

Price exchanged clothes with Knox through the bars. The sheriff then turned back to Thompson, urgency in his eyes.

"Wrap that blanket around you. Go sit in that cell and cover your head."

Thompson nodded without hesitation. As he moved to the cell, Price turned to Jailer Graves.

"Go to the door and stall. They want the prisoner. Make them think you aren't going to hand him over."

Graves looked terrified, his eyes wide, but he nodded reluctantly.

"Then," Price added, "I want you to loudly tell them that you're going to bring the prisoner out. The guys around back should run to the front. Me and Knox are going to make a run for it while you bring out Thompson."

Graves swallowed hard. "What if it doesn't work? They might shoot me."

"Damnit, Adam," Price snapped. "They aren't going to shoot you, but the governor will make life hell for me and you both if those men kill the prisoner."

Graves nodded quickly. "Yes, sir."

Price turned back to Knox's cell, his voice filled with a sense of urgency as he spoke.

"They're coming to lynch you," he said, his expression dark. "We've got to get you out of here. Come with me!"

But as Price attempted to open the cell door, he

realized it was locked. Panic set in, and the noise from the mob outside grew louder. Other prisoners, terrified for their own safety, began shouting from their cells.

"Give me the key, Adam!" Price demanded, his hand outstretched.

Graves threw the keys to Price, who scrambled to unlock the door. When the cell door finally opened, Knox bolted out but stood frozen for a moment, unsure of where to go next.

"Come with me!" Price shouted urgently.

The banging on the door grew louder, the mob's impatience becoming more frantic. Knox quickly joined Price by a side door.

Graves, still holding a rifle, walked cautiously to the front door, his heart racing.

He opened it slowly, looking out at the mob.

"What do you want?" Graves called out, trying to keep his voice steady.

"You know why we're here," one of the mob members said, his voice cold and determined. "Turn over the Bell's Bend killer. We know he was captured earlier today."

Graves hesitated, his face pale. "You know I can't do that. I could lose my job!" he stammered.

"We don't want to hurt you," the mob member said, his voice dangerously calm. "But we're taking him dead or alive. Preferably alive, for now…"

Graves glanced back over at Thompson, who was sitting in the cell with his head covered by the blanket. Thompson nodded, signaling that he was ready.

Price and Knox stood by the side door, ready to make their escape.

"Alright, alright," Graves said loudly, trying to buy

them time. "Let me get my keys. I don't want any trouble. Give me a second."

He quickly closed the front door, his hands trembling as he grabbed the keys. Price cracked open the side door, peeking out into the night.

"Let's go! Let's go!" Price hissed at Knox, his voice full of urgency.

As Graves walked back to the front door with Thompson, Price and Knox dashed through the dark streets, desperate to escape the chaos and the fury of the mob.

Hearts racing and nearly out of breath, Price and Knox darted into the woods behind the jail. The branches of the trees rustled softly in the night air, masking their movements, but the tension in their chests made each step feel heavier than the last. Price dropped to a crouch instinctively, his training taking over, but Knox stood still for a moment, exposed in the open.

"What are you doing? Get down!" Price barked, his voice low but urgent.

Knox snapped out of his stupor, dropping to the ground beside Price. They lay in silence, watching the shadows of the night, their breaths shallow, their muscles tense, listening to the distant sounds of the mob as they gathered around the front of the jail.

♦ ♦ ♦ ♦ ♦ ♦

Back inside, Jailer Graves led Thompson to the door of the jail. The mob, pressing in from the outside, had already surrounded the front door. One of the men, a large figure with a thick beard, shoved his way forward and grabbed Thompson, ripping the blanket off him with a quick, rough motion.

"This ain't the killer!" the man shouted, his voice thick with frustration.

Graves froze for a moment, unsure of what to say, as panic spread through the air. He stammered, trying to explain.

"This is the only man we have being held for murder," Graves said, his voice wavering with uncertainty.

The mob, growing more restless, pushed into the jail, moving quickly from cell to cell. They examined the prisoners, some of them muttering under their breath as they searched for the man they believed had committed the murders.

Outside, Sheriff Price and Knox huddled in the shadows, watching the mob slowly disperse. The streets fell quiet, and Knox dared not move until he was certain it was safe.

When it seemed the coast was clear, they made their move. They sprinted through the woods, hearts pounding, the fear of being caught driving them forward. But as they reached the edge of the trees, Price's foot caught on a rock, and he tripped, collapsing to the ground with a sharp grunt.

"Damnit, my ankle." Price's voice was strained, pain quickly flashing across his face.

Knox froze, his chest tight, looking ahead at the path that could lead him to freedom—and at the injured sheriff behind him.

He hesitated for a moment, weighing his options. The sound of the mob still echoed in his mind, but the sight of Price struggling to get up made Knox's decision clear.

He ran back, kneeling next to Price and helping him to his feet.

"Come on, Sheriff," Knox urged, his voice filled with determination.

Wincing in pain, Price leaned on Knox for support. He was visibly hurt, but he nodded, a grim resolve settling over him. Together, they limped down a narrow side street, their progress slow but steady.

"Where are we going?" Knox asked, his voice filled with concern.

Price, his face strained but resolute, pointed down the road.

"The governor's mansion isn't far from here. I hate to disturb him this late, but he'll know what to do."

# Breakfast with the Governor

Sheriff Price and Knox stood before the imposing Governor's mansion, the grand columns of the building rising high against the dark sky. The mansion exuded wealth and power, every inch carefully manicured, its elegance undeniable. Price paused for a moment as he rubbed his sore ankle. Knox, standing beside him, felt the tension building, his nerves twitching from everything that had happened that night.

Price glanced at Knox and then reached into his pocket, pulling out a set of cold, iron handcuffs. He looked at Knox for a moment, his face hard but sympathetic.

"I'm going to have to put these on you if we're going to see the governor," Price said.

Knox nodded silently, resigned. "Yes, sir. I understand."

The mansion's front doors were thick and solid, their grandiose design matching the power and wealth that lay behind them. As the sharp knock echoed through the house, it shattered the stillness of the lavish interior.

From the upstairs bedroom, Governor Albert Marks, a short, stocky man with a long, brown beard, stumbled out, his feet shuffling sluggishly across the marble floors. He rubbed his eyes, still groggy, and peered out the window. Seeing no sign of danger, but sensing urgency, he hurried to the door. The moment he opened it, he was met with the unexpected—Sheriff Price standing on his doorstep, accompanied by a prisoner.

"John?" Marks muttered, his voice thick with sleep.

"I'm really sorry, Governor," Price said, stepping

inside. His voice was edged with strain, tension riding every word.

Marks, still blinking away the sleep, looked at the two men, confusion settling in. "What's going on?"

Price, stepping further into the hallway, didn't waste time with pleasantries. "This is Knox Martin. We arrested him for the murders in Bell's Bend yesterday."

Knox stood a bit straighter, despite the handcuffs that clinked at his wrists. He looked Marks in the eyes, offering a strained smile.

"Good evening, sir. Or is it morning?" Knox said, his voice thick with exhaustion.

Marks gave a polite but tight smile, the frustration of being roused so suddenly clear in his eyes. He didn't return the smile. "What is all this?" Marks said, clearly bewildered.

"A large group came to lynch him, but we got him out just in time," Price explained, his tone curt but tired.

From somewhere deep in the mansion, a voice called out, alarmed.

"Who is it? What is the matter?"

Marks groaned in frustration, rubbing his forehead. "It's the sheriff, dear," he called back, stepping aside to let Price and Knox into the parlor.

Sheriff Price limped to the side, motioning for the governor to join him in a quiet corner of the room. He lowered his voice.

"I'm sorry, Albert," Price said, serious and weary. "I just didn't know what to do or where to take him. If anyone sees him, he's a dead man."

Marks studied Price for a moment. His eyes flicked between the sheriff and the prisoner, before settling back on Price.

"You did the right thing," Marks said finally, his voice steady but full of authority. "An angry mob doesn't get to dictate his fate. He very well may hang, but he'll have his day in court. In the morning, I can go to the capitol and arrange to have him transported to a safe location. I'm thinking maybe Murfreesboro or Gallatin."

Marks paused, eyeing Price closely. The man looked worn down, his shoulders sagging and his skin pale beneath the lanternlight.

"How tired are you?" Marks asked, his tone softening.

Price wiped his face with one hand, trying to keep upright. "It's been a long night, but I'm fine. What exactly do you have in mind?"

Marks stepped back slightly, thinking it over.

"If you can stay awake until the sun comes up," he said, "you and the prisoner can hide out in the carriage house."

Price, already feeling the pull of sleep, blinked hard. "Yes, sir. I'll keep an eye on him."

Marks' eyes softened slightly as he watched him.

"You're okay, right? I can make you some coffee," he offered gently.

Price shook his head, already turning toward the door. "No, thank you. I'll take the prisoner back there. We'll be fine until the morning."

The two men moved through the cold, damp air that wrapped around the carriage house. The silence pressed in from every side, broken only by the creaking of old wood and the muffled sounds of their footsteps. Dim light filtered through the cracked windows. The air carried the faint smells of leather and hay and the cool earth below.

Sheriff Price and Knox sat against opposite walls, backs pressed to the wood. Price gripped his pistol loosely, the metal firm in his tired hands. His eyelids sagged as exhaustion overtook him, dragging his mind closer to sleep.

And still, neither man spoke.

Knox, on the other hand, seemed wide awake. Every muscle in his body was tense, every inch of him wound tight like a coiled spring, his eyes darting from corner to corner. He couldn't shake the feeling that something was coming for him, that the walls might close in at any moment.

"Just a couple more hours," Price murmured, his voice rough from lack of sleep. "And we'll find a secure place to keep you."

Knox nodded, his body still restless as he shifted on the floor. He didn't know if he could trust that.

"Thank you for taking such good care of me back at the jail," Knox said quietly, his voice breaking the heavy silence.

Price's gaze lingered on Knox for a moment longer than necessary. He was studying him, not just the man before him but the story that lay behind those tired, nervous eyes. There was suspicion, but more than that, there was curiosity — something Price couldn't quite place.

"Why didn't you just run?" Price's question was simple, but it cut through the tension, pulling Knox's gaze toward him.

Knox tilted his head, meeting the sheriff's eyes before looking away again. He hesitated, his fingers tapping nervously on his knees.

"You was hurt," he said finally, as though the

answer was obvious.

Price smirked, a dry chuckle escaping his lips.

"Y'all would've caught me eventually."

The sheriff nodded, his eyes glinting with reluctant admiration. "You're probably right. But I do appreciate you coming back to help me."

There was a long moment of silence, thick with the unspoken questions neither of them had the answer to. Price wasn't sure he understood Knox. Something about him didn't add up. How eager he was to run, only to return when the sheriff needed help—there was a certain kind of honesty in that, but also a deep confusion.

"You killed that couple on that farm, didn't you?" Price asked, the words heavy as they left his mouth.

Knox's shoulders slumped. He closed his eyes briefly, taking a long, shaky breath, and then nodded.

"Yeah, I did."

"Why'd you do it?" Price pressed, his voice low, trying to understand.

Knox let out a long, shaky breath. "He owed me some money, and he was wanting to kill me."

Price's brows wrinkled. "Kill you?"

"Aunt Mary told me so."

Price shook his head. "Aunt Mary? Is that lady really your aunt?"

Knox hesitated for a moment, then looked the sheriff in the eye. "No sir. She grew up with my momma in Alabama. When I came up here looking for work, Momma told me she'd let me stay with her. I been staying with her for about a year before Mr. Whittemeyer brought me on."

Price processed the words, trying to piece the story together. "How'd she know the man you killed?"

Knox's face was serious now, as though he was telling a truth that Price might never understand.

"She saw him in her visions. She said there was something evil about him."

Price let out a long sigh, his frustration mounting. "Son, that's all hogwash."

Knox, as if to prove something to himself more than to Price, reached up and fingered the gris-gris around his neck, the small necklace hanging there. He rubbed it between his fingers, the touch soothing in some strange, inexplicable way.

"She gave me this for protection. Seems like it's working pretty good so far," Knox said, his voice quiet but filled with an unshakeable conviction.

Price snorted, a soft chuckle escaping him as he tried to stay awake, the weariness settling deeper in his bones. His head leaned back against the wall, and his eyelids fluttered as the night's events replayed in his mind. He wasn't sure what to make of Knox—the kid was a mystery, a puzzle that didn't quite fit together. Every answer Knox gave raised more questions, and it gnawed at Price. But his exhaustion was overwhelming, and as he sat in the dim light of the carriage house, he felt his body give in to the pull of sleep. His thoughts drifted, and soon enough, the quiet of the night eventually took him under.

◆ ◆ ◆ ◆ ◆ ◆

The first rays of dawn broke through the cracks in the carriage house, casting pale light across the dusty floor. The world outside was waking up, but inside, the air was still thick with the remnants of the night.

Price stirred slowly, his purple ankle making every movement feel more painful than it should have. He blinked a few times, still groggy from the restless sleep he'd managed to steal. The cold of the night hadn't quite left his bones, and his muscles ached from the tension he had held throughout the hours of stillness.

But something was wrong. Price's eyes snapped open when he realized that Knox was standing over him. The young man was handcuffed, his posture steady and controlled. But what made Price's heart skip a beat was the sight of the pistol—his pistol—in Knox's hand. The cold steel gleamed in the early morning light, and for a moment, Price's mind went blank.

Panic rushed through him, his heartbeat quickening as fear crept up his spine. He froze, staring at Knox, unable to move. His hands twitched with the instinct to defend himself, but he couldn't make his body obey. All he could do was watch as Knox stepped closer, his footsteps unnervingly calm.

Knox's gaze was steady. He didn't look like a man in control of a dangerous situation. Instead, he seemed… calm, too calm. Price could feel the cold sweat breaking out across his skin, his body tense and still.

Then, Knox spoke.

"Sheriff, you dropped this while you were sleeping." The words were simple, but they were enough to rattle Price to his core.

Knox extended the pistol toward him, and for a moment, Price didn't move. His heart raced, and his mind was a jumble of confusion and adrenaline. What was happening?

Price's hand moved of its own accord, trembling slightly as he reached out to take the gun from Knox. The cold metal felt heavier than it should, and his fingers wrapped around it hesitantly. He glanced up at Knox, trying to make sense of the situation, but the young man's face remained neutral, as though the gun wasn't in his hand at all.

"Uh, thank you," Price muttered, still trying to process what had just happened. He didn't know if he should be relieved or terrified. The calmness in Knox's demeanor only made the situation more confusing.

Knox didn't offer much in response. He simply stepped back, allowing Price a moment to collect himself. The sheriff didn't quite know what to say.

"You want to go see if the governor is up?" Price finally asked, his voice rough with exhaustion.

Knox smiled, the faintest curve of his lips. A small moment of connection in the midst of everything that had happened.

"Here. You need some help getting up?" Knox extended his bound hands.

Price hesitated for a moment, then took Knox's hands. He pulled himself up with the younger man's assistance, his legs stiff and sore from the long night.

They walked toward the door but neither of them said anything. The silence was thick between them, but it wasn't uncomfortable. It was just the quiet understanding that they had both survived the night—barely.

As they reached the door, Price glanced over at Knox, a tired smile tugging at his lips despite the situation.

"Oh yeah, I would appreciate it if you didn't mention me falling asleep to the governor," Price said with a soft chuckle.

Knox smiled in return, the smallest hint of amusement in his eyes.

"Yes, sir," Knox replied softly.

♦ ♦ ♦ ♦ ♦ ♦

In the daylight the Governor's mansion was as grand as one would expect—a towering structure that reflected the wealth and power of its occupants. Inside, it was even more opulent. Fine tapestries adorned the walls, and the furnishings were upholstered in rich fabrics, the wood polished to a gleaming finish. The air in the dining room was heavy with the scent of expensive wood and a faint hint of cologne.

Sheriff Price, Knox, and Governor Marks sat around a large table. A basket of fruit rested in the center. Marks had insisted they sit, though it was clear he wasn't quite comfortable with the presence of a prisoner in his home.

The governor picked up an apple and took a bite, his sharp gaze moving between Knox and Price. He chewed slowly, as though trying to make sense of the situation.

"Would you like some fruit?" he asked, breaking the silence with a casualness that felt strange in the moment.

Knox, who had been eyeing a peach in the basket, hesitated. The hunger in his stomach was almost unbearable, but he didn't feel quite right taking something so simple while in such a strange position. His eyes flicked to the peach again, and for a moment, he thought about reaching for it.

"No, thank you," Price replied, his voice gravelly with fatigue.

Knox's fingers twitched towards the peach, but he paused. He wasn't sure if he had the right to just take it, even with the invitation. He was a prisoner, after all. But the hunger gnawed at him, and his eyes lingered on the fruit.

Noticing his hesitation, Governor Marks gave him a small nod. "Go on ahead, son. Help yourself."

It was a simple gesture, but it felt like a release. Knox's hand moved quickly, almost instinctively, and he grabbed the peach. He bit into it immediately, the sweet juice dribbling down his chin as he savored the bite. It was the first real taste of food he'd had in what felt like days, and the relief that washed over him was almost overwhelming. For a moment, he let himself forget the circumstances, the charges hanging over his head, the fear of what was to come.

Marks watched him with a mixture of curiosity and mild distaste, though his expression softened when he turned his attention back to Price. He cleared his throat before speaking again, his voice shifting to something more businesslike.

"Once I get to the capitol, I'll make arrangements for you to be taken to the Sumner County jail in Gallatin," Marks explained, his gaze now fixed on Knox. "The people there won't be as excited as they are here, and we'll be able to keep you safe. I want you and the sheriff to sit tight until someone comes for you."

Marks rose from his seat, his chair scraping slightly

against the floor, and Knox followed the movement with his eyes. This was real. His fate was being decided in this room, and though the governor's tone was calm, there was no mistaking the gravity in his words.

"We're going to get you your day in court," Marks continued, his expression hardening slightly. "But you've been accused of two very serious crimes. If the jury says we have to hang you, then we have to hang you. I hope you understand."

Knox bowed his head, his gaze dropping to the table. He didn't speak, not knowing how to respond, and the room fell into a heavy silence.

Governor Marks turned toward Price then, as though dismissing the conversation, his voice softening.

"You and the prisoner just stay here for a while," Marks said, motioning to the space around them. "Novella can make you some breakfast."

The door to the room opened, and Novella Marks, a woman in her fifties with a well-maintained composure, entered, carrying two plates of food. Her eyes briefly flicked to Knox, and the discomfort in her gaze was evident. She had not expected to see a prisoner in her home, and though she hid it well, the tension in her posture suggested otherwise. Still, she placed the plates on the table with a professional grace.

"Ham and eggs okay?" she asked, her voice warm but with an edge of unease.

Price, who hadn't eaten properly in hours, nodded gratefully. "Yes, ma'am."

Feeling his stomach growl louder than before, Knox quietly added, "Yes, ma'am. Thank you."

Novella nodded curtly and quickly exited, her footsteps fading down the hall. The two men were left in silence.

Price reached for an apple, his hands a little more eager than usual without the governor present, and took a hearty bite. His body had been running on adrenaline for so long that the sudden relief of food was almost overwhelming.

Knox, too, reached for another peach with quiet hunger. For a fleeting second, it felt almost normal again, like he was just a man at a table having breakfast, instead of a prisoner facing an uncertain future.

# The Trial

The morning was cool, and the streets outside Davidson County Courthouse were packed with a restless crowd, eager to see the man who had made headlines across the state. The horse-drawn wagon creaked as it rolled down the cobblestone street, flanked by four armed deputies. The wagon's wheels groaned with each turn, and the air was filled with the low hum of whispered conversation. A sea of people pressed in from all sides, their eyes fixed on the man sitting inside — the notorious Knox Martin, accused of murdering John and Emily Whittemeyer.

The crowd was eager, but their eagerness was dark, driven by a mix of fear and anger. People craned their necks to get a glimpse of the infamous killer, their whispers thick with judgment. Knox's heart pounded in his chest as he looked around. Their glares were burning into him, sharp and accusing. He could hear the murmurs — the Bells Bend killer, the murderer. He swallowed hard, his body stiff, as the deputies moved quickly to escort him inside. Every step he took was weighed down with the knowledge that every person in this crowd knew his name, knew his face.

Once inside, the courthouse was a quiet contrast to the chaos outside. The heavy silence inside the small courtroom felt suffocating. Judge James Quarles, an older man with a no-nonsense demeanor, sat at the bench. He looked over the proceedings with a practiced air, his sharp eyes scanning every person in the room. At Knox's side stood District Attorney Anthony Long, whose crisp suit and rigid posture suggested a man prepared for a quick, easy case. But there was no denying the tension in the air.

Judge Quarles tapped his gavel once, his voice ringing out, cold and authoritative.

"This seems to be a very simple case," he said, his gaze moving between Knox and Long.

Anthony Long nodded firmly. "Yes, your honor. Mr. Martin has pled guilty to the murder of John and Emily Whittemeyer."

Knox didn't raise his head, his eyes focused on the floor, his hands bound tightly in front of him. The weight of Long's words pressed on his chest. Guilty. The word echoed in his mind.

The momentary stillness was broken by the sound of the courtroom door swinging open. There was a flurry of movement as Josiah Taylor, a smooth-talking, ambitious lawyer in his forties, hurried into the room. His suit was sharply pressed, and a confident smile was plastered on his face as he made his way toward the front. He was brimming with the kind of energy that immediately drew the attention of everyone in the room.

"Good morning, your honor," Taylor said, his voice smooth, his confidence clear. He turned to Anthony Long with a quick nod. "Hello, Mr. Long. I'm Josiah Taylor. I'm here to represent Mr. Martin."

The suddenness of his arrival threw the courtroom into confusion. Judge Quarles raised an eyebrow, his face a mask of irritation, and Long shifted uncomfortably beside him. It was clear this was an unexpected turn.

Taylor, unfazed by the confusion, continued, "It's my understanding that Mr. Martin has not been represented in this proceeding. Is that correct?"

Grinding his teeth slightly, Judge Quarles turned his eyes to Knox. "Is this man your attorney?" he asked, his voice laced with skepticism.

Knox blinked, his mind racing. He hadn't hired anyone. He didn't have money for a lawyer, yet this man was here, claiming to represent him. The whole situation felt surreal. He trusted the lawyer's confident demeanor, unsure of what else to do. He nodded, his confusion evident but his trust implicit in the moment.

"I didn't hire no attorney," Knox muttered quietly, still trying to process the situation. "I ain't got no money. I can't pay you."

"It's alright," Taylor replied, his tone reassuring. "Your Aunt Mary hired me. Just let me do all the talking in here. I don't want you to say anything. Do you understand?"

Knox's brow furrowed in confusion, his mind still grappling with everything happening around him. He looked at Taylor for a long moment, unsure what to make of this man's sudden appearance.

"I'm a guilty man..." Knox started, the words falling from his mouth as if they had been waiting to be said.

Taylor didn't flinch, his expression unwavering. "Did anyone see you at the murder scene?"

Knox hesitated, thinking back. He hadn't been seen, and the thought brought him a small sense of clarity in the chaos.

"No, sir," he answered quietly.

"That's exactly what I wanted to hear." Taylor's voice was steady, authoritative. "You let me do the talking. Understand?"

Knox gave him a blank look, unsure but too tired to question him further. He nodded, though his thoughts were clouded. Taylor's energy, though, was contagious. There was no doubt that this man had a plan.

In the next moment, Taylor was darting forward, moving to the bench with a sense of urgency.

"Your honor," he said, his voice carrying easily to the judge. "My client would like to plead not guilty."

The room went silent, the air thick with shock. Judge Quarles's face flushed red, and District Attorney Long stormed toward the bench, frustration written all over his features.

"He's already confessed," Long snapped, his voice harsh, but Taylor was unfazed.

"Was it coerced?" Taylor asked, his voice calm but pointed.

Long's jaw tightened as he walked back to his seat, shaking his head. The room was full of tension now, the air crackling with the friction between the defense and prosecution.

Judge Quarles, still seething with irritation, spoke after a moment of silence. "Alright, we will have to empanel a jury."

He turned to Deputy Jim Norris, who had been sitting quietly in the back of the courtroom and motioned for him to come forward. Norris stood quickly and approached the bench, his face a mask of professionalism.

"What can I do for you, sir?" Norris asked.

Quarles scribbled something quickly on a piece of paper and handed it to Norris. "I'm going to need forty-two men back here tomorrow by 2 p.m. so we can fill out the jury."

Norris nodded, taking the paper without hesitation. "Yes, sir," he replied, quickly exiting the courtroom.

As the doors of the courtroom swung open behind him, the tension lingered, thick and heavy in the air. The room was now silent, but the preparations were underway. As the judge exited, Long kicked a chair, sending it crashing across the courtroom. Taylor snickered as Knox raised an eyebrow, a hint of unease creeping into him.

◆ ◆ ◆ ◆ ◆ ◆

A few days later, the courtroom buzzed with anticipation as the jury filed into their seats. The room was thick with tension, the kind of silence that fills the air before a storm. The judge's gavel slammed down with authority, silencing the room completely. Judge Quarles wasted no time in getting the proceedings started, his voice cutting through the stillness.

"Call your first witness."

The State wasted no time either, bringing forward Abe Hewland, the ferry operator. His eyes, though tired from age, held a quiet confidence as he made his way to the stand. His movements were slow, deliberate, but there was a calmness about him that filled the room with a certain quiet respect. He took a seat and adjusted himself, glancing around the courtroom as if taking it all in for the first time.

The murmur of conversation died down as Scott Singer, the eager young reporter, shifted in his seat near the back of the room, his eyes flicking to Aunt Mary, who sat just a few rows away. The old woman's eyes never left Abe Hewland, her fingers gently rubbing an odd, feathered charm hanging from her neck. The courtroom felt heavy with her presence, as if something unseen was watching everyone.

Judge Quarles nodded toward the witness stand, his voice firm. "Mr. Hewland, please state your name for the record."

The old man's voice was soft but steady. "Abraham Sidney Hewland."

District Attorney Long stood, his stance rigid as he approached the witness stand. His voice was clear and practiced as he addressed Abe.

"Mr. Hewland, what do you do for a living?"

Abe cleared his throat, his weathered hands resting on the arms of the chair. "I operate the ferry over on Bell's Bend."

"On the evening of the murder, how many times did you see Knox Martin?" Long continued, his tone steady, as though the case was already decided.

Abe thought for a moment, his eyes drifting as he recalled the events. "I saw him twice."

"Can you tell me about the first time you saw him?" Long pressed, his gaze unwavering.

Abe's memory shifted back to that evening. "It was about 6:30. It was startin' to get dark, and I was about to go inside to get a bite to eat when I saw Knox waving at me from the other side of the river. I went back inside, took my beans off the stove, and then I went over and brought him across."

"Could you tell if he was headed to the Whittemeyer farm?" Long asked, his pen hovering above his notepad.

Abe nodded. "John's farm was about a hundred yards from where I dropped him off. I believe so, but he didn't say where he was goin'."

"Can you tell me what you were doing at 10 o'clock that night?" Long asked, his voice shifting slightly, probing for more details.

Abe chuckled softly. "I was asleep!"

The courtroom seemed to hold its breath as Long's next question came quickly. "Did something wake you up?"

Abe didn't hesitate, recalling the disruption with ease. "Why, yes. I heard someone bangin' on my door. So, I got up to see what all the fuss was about."

"What was the fuss about?" Long pressed, eager for more details.

Abe's face darkened slightly as he remembered the confusion of the moment. "When I opened the door, there was Knox, standin' there wearin' John's black coat."

"John?" Long asked, his brow furrowing in confusion.

"John Whittemeyer," Abe clarified.

"Did you notice anything else about Mr. Martin's appearance?" Long asked, leaning forward slightly.

Abe didn't miss a beat. "He looked like he'd been in a tussle. His clothes were all out of sorts, and there was blood on his face. He was breathin' heavy, real heavy."

The jury began to whisper to each other, their eyes shifting between the witness and Knox, who sat motionless, his hands clenched tightly. The tension in the air felt thick, suffocating.

Long continued, undeterred by the rising murmurs. "Mr. Hewland, why was Mr. Martin knocking on your door?"

Abe scratched his chin thoughtfully. "He told me he needed to get across the river. I tried to tell him I could take him across in the mornin', but he insisted. That young man was pretty persistent."

"Did you take him across?" Long asked, his voice almost mechanical now, as if he were running through a checklist.

Abe's eyes flicked to the jury for a brief moment before he nodded. "Of course. He handed me five dollars!"

"Did you have a conversation with Mr. Martin as you crossed the river?"

Abe's lips curled slightly, as though the memory of it amused him. "No. He seemed real jumpy, so I didn't bother him. Once we got to the other side, he took off runnin' like his trousers were on fire."

Long nodded and turned back to the judge. "Your honor, I have no further questions for this witness."

Abe stood slowly from the witness stand, giving one last glance around the courtroom before he shuffled toward the exit. His eyes met Aunt Mary's once again, and for a brief moment. Her stare seemed to pierce through him. She was stroking the charm around her neck, her gaze steady and unwavering.

Before Abe could leave, Josiah Taylor, Knox's defense attorney, rose from his seat with the grace of a man who was used to having the floor. He moved across the courtroom with confidence, his presence filling the room with a sense of control. His smile was wide, but his eyes were calculating as he approached Abe.

"Mr. Hewland," Taylor began, his voice smooth, almost too smooth. "You said that my client woke you at 10 o'clock, correct?"

Abe nodded, a slight frown crossing his face as he sat back down. "Yes."

"So, at that late hour, it would've been pretty dark out, right?" Taylor continued, his tone polite, though there was a sharpness to his words that suggested he was about to challenge the testimony.

Abe sighed, clearly growing impatient. "Well, yeah, but there was a full moon that night, reflectin' off the river. It looked to me like Knox had been in a fight."

Taylor smiled, the glint in his eye reflecting a quiet victory. "Even with a full moon, it still would've been difficult to say with 100% certainty that the jacket Mr. Martin was wearing was John Whittemeyer's, wouldn't you agree?"

Abe's patience was thinning, and his irritation was evident in his voice. "Son, John took my ferry across that river hundreds of times. There's a tear in the right arm of his jacket that caused his elbow to pop up sometimes. I didn't really realize it 'til Knox and I got on the boat, but you can see it as clear as day, even at night."

Knox squirmed in his seat, his nerves starting to get the better of him. The tension in the courtroom grew with each passing moment.

Taylor's questions continued, his tone smooth and unrelenting. "Tell me, Mr. Hewland, was it uncommon for you to carry Mr. Martin across the river?"

Abe's response came quickly, without hesitation. "Not really. He had an aunt or a grandmother on the other side, I think. Seems like I took him across a few times."

Taylor leaned in, as though pressing his advantage. "Do you think, on that night, Knox simply wanted to visit his relative?"

Before Abe could respond, District Attorney Long was on his feet, his voice sharp. "Objection!"

Judge Quarles raised his hand to silence the room. "Mr. Taylor, do you have any more questions for Mr. Hewland before I excuse him?"

Taylor looked at the judge and shook his head. "No, your honor."

The judge nodded toward Abe. "Mr. Hewland, thank you. You're excused."

Abe made his way back to his seat, his steps slow but steady. As he passed Aunt Mary, he caught the intensity of her gaze. She didn't break her stare, her fingers still lightly stroking the feathered charm, her focus unyielding.

District Attorney Anthony Long stood, his voice cutting through the silence as he called for the next witness. "The state calls Patton Foster."

The door to the witness stand creaked as Patton Foster walked up, his face drawn, a man who had clearly seen more than his fair share of sorrow. His dark eyes were tired, but there was still a sharpness to his gaze as he turned to face the courtroom.

Long was ready with his questions. "Sir, can you please state your full name for the record?"

Patton nodded stiffly, his voice thick but steady. "Patton Gregory Foster."

Long continued, the questions coming one after the other. "Can you tell us your relationship with the Whittemeyers?"

Patton paused, the question hanging in the air for a moment. "Uh, yes. Emily Whittemeyer was my sister. John Whittemeyer was my brother-in-law."

The words came out slowly, as if saying them made the loss feel all the more real.

"Can you tell us what you were doing on the morning of January 17th?" Long pressed, his voice hard with the urgency of the case.

Patton took a deep breath before answering. "I stopped by Emily and John's farm to get some eggs and to borrow a plow."

Long's voice softened as he continued, sensing the sadness in Patton's tone. "I know this is difficult, but can you please tell us what happened when you arrived at the Whittemeyer farm?"

Patton's chest tightened as he exhaled slowly, blinking back the threat of tears. His voice faltered as he spoke. "When I pulled up, I walked up to the cabin. I knocked, but no one answered. I called out for my sister. When she didn't come to the door, I went inside."

His face began to tighten, the emotion overwhelming him. "I heard Johnny cryin', and I thought it was strange, 'cause Emily was always so attentive to him. I was shocked to see that she and John were still sleepin'. She always got up early and made a big breakfast."

Patton wiped at his eyes, but the tears wouldn't stop. The pain of that morning, so fresh and raw, was pouring out, no matter how much he tried to hold it back.

"I walked closer to the bed and noticed some blood on John's pillow," Patton continued, his voice trembling now. "Then it hit me. Something was really wrong. They were both dead."

A deep sob racked his body, and he struggled to speak. "I picked up my nephew and went to get help."

The air in the courtroom seemed to evaporate, the quiet tension pressing down on everyone. Even Knox, sitting at the defense table, knew without a doubt that he was doomed.

Judge Quarles cleared his throat. "Mr. Foster, we can take a recess."

"No," Patton replied quickly, shaking his head. "No. I'm okay. We can continue."

Long nodded, then turned toward the judge, signaling the end of his questioning. "I don't have any further questions, your honor."

But before the court could move on, Josiah Taylor, Knox's defense attorney, rose from his seat. His smile was confident, almost smug, as he made his way to the stand. He glanced at Patton, his expression shifting to one of mock sympathy.

"Mr. Foster," Taylor began, his voice dripping with a feigned sorrow. "You have my deepest condolences. What you saw that morning was horrible. I'm pained by your loss."

Patton gritted his teeth, his jaw tightening as Taylor's words rang in his ears. He forced himself to nod, though his face betrayed his anger.

"Sir, were you aware of your sister and her husband's financial problems?" Taylor's question came with the smoothness of a seasoned lawyer, but the sharp edge was evident.

Patton looked at him for a moment, then shook his head. "Uh, no sir."

Judge Quarles slammed his gavel down, his face a mask of irritation. "I've heard enough. Mr. Foster, you are dismissed."

Patton, his face a mixture of grief and frustration, stood up slowly. As he left the stand, Aunt Mary watched him with her unblinking gaze, her fingers still stroking the feathered charm. Her stare followed him until he exited the courtroom, and though her expression didn't change, there was something unsettling in the way she regarded him.

Taylor, with his usual smug confidence, walked back to the defense table, his head held high, as though the day's events had unfolded exactly as he'd expected. Judge Quarles, however, could only watch as the courtroom settled into a tense silence, the future of Knox Martin hanging on the edge of every word.

District Attorney Anthony Long was quick to call the next witness. "I'd like to call Detective William Thompson."

The room was still as Detective Thompson made his way to the stand. He was known for his no-nonsense demeanor and sharp mind. As he sat, his eyes scanned the courtroom with the authority of someone who had seen it all. Long stood to address him, his voice steady and purposeful.

"Detective, can you please tell the gentlemen of the jury what Mr. Martin told you on the night of January 20th?"

Thompson nodded slightly. "Yes, Mr. Martin confessed to me that he killed the Whittemeyers."

There was a ripple of murmurs in the room, but Thompson continued without pause.

"Did he tell you how he killed them?"

Thompson's eyes never wavered as he answered, his voice low but clear. "He told me that he struck them both with a wagon spoke and then threw it into the fireplace. Naturally, we were not able to recover the murder weapon."

A heavy silence settled over the courtroom as the jury absorbed the information. Knox sat at the defense table, his face pale, his jaw tight. Aunt Mary, seated just behind him, stroked the charm around her neck, her face taut with tension.

Long wasn't finished. "Did Mr. Martin explain why he killed them?"

Thompson hesitated, as though unsure how to frame his answer. "The defendant explained to me that John Whittemeyer owed him some money. He also implied that a dark spiritual force compelled him to kill John and his wife."

The words hung in the air like a dark omen. The crowd seemed to shift uneasily at the mention of the supernatural. Knox's heart sank at the weight of the statement. Aunt Mary remained eerily quiet, her hands now still, her eyes narrowing as she watched Thompson intently.

Long turned to the judge. "I don't have any further questions, your honor."

Judge Quarles nodded, then turned to Josiah Taylor, Knox's defense attorney. "Mr. Taylor?"

Taylor rose slowly, his movements smooth, almost too calm for the tense atmosphere of the room. His confident smile was a stark contrast to the gravity of the situation. He crossed the room to stand before the witness stand, his voice carrying easily to every corner of the courtroom.

"So, Detective Thompson," Taylor began, his tone laced with an edge of subtle challenge. "You admit that you were unable to find the murder weapon?"

Thompson responded, his tone even. "Not exactly. We did search the fireplace and found a charred wooden nub that may have been part of the spoke that Knox used to beat the two victims."

Taylor nodded as if the response was expected, then pressed on. "As far as the confession goes... did Mr. Martin have an attorney present when you spoke with him?"

Thompson's brow furrowed slightly. "No. He did not request one."

Taylor didn't miss a beat. "Would you say the confession was made under duress?"

Thompson paused, his eyes never leaving Taylor. "I think Mr. Martin was experiencing quite a bit of stress after being arrested, but he seemed to be coherent and forthcoming when I questioned him."

Taylor's smile tightened, as though he was carefully crafting his next point. "Tell me this, Detective. Could you hear the mob approaching the police station that night, inside his cell?"

Thompson hesitated for a moment before answering. "I believe we did hear them, but it was after he had already confessed."

Taylor's voice dropped, a bit of sarcasm creeping into his words. "If I knew a mob was coming to lynch me, I might say just about anything to get the protection I needed."

Judge Quarles raised an eyebrow. "Is that a question, Mr. Taylor?"

"No, your honor," Taylor responded smoothly, his grin unwavering.

Quarles narrowed his eyes but said nothing. After a moment, he turned to Thompson. "Do you have any more questions?"

Taylor shook his head. "No, your honor."

The judge sighed, clearly frustrated by the back-and-forth. "Mr. Taylor, will your client be taking the stand in his own defense?"

All eyes shifted to Knox, who glanced over at Josiah Taylor. The young lawyer's confident expression faltered for just a moment before he spoke, his voice steady.

"No, your honor," Taylor said firmly. "My client is a simple man who was raised without an education. I'm not going to allow the prosecutor to try to trick him into incriminating himself any further on the witness stand. Knox Martin will not be testifying."

Judge Quarles rolled his eyes, his frustration evident. "I believe we have heard enough for the day. Let's reconvene in the morning at 8. If the jury has reached a decision, we can announce a verdict."

With a sharp bang, the judge's gavel slammed down, signaling the end of the day's proceedings. Knox rose from his seat, his body stiff with tension, and was escorted from the courtroom by Deputy Norris.

The courtroom was silent as Knox walked out. He didn't know what the next day would bring, but he knew the walls were closing in, and no matter what, he would have to face the consequences of his actions.

Later that night, Knox sat alone in the holding cell, the walls around him feeling like they were closing in. The room was dimly lit, with only a small window letting in a sliver of pale moonlight. His hands were clasped tightly in his lap. He stared at the cold, stone floor, his thoughts running wild, trapped in a cycle of fear and regret.

The sound of boots on the floor broke the silence, and Sheriff Price appeared in front of the bars, his face grim. He studied Knox for a long moment, his expression hard but not unkind. Price didn't speak at first, just stood there, looking at the young man.

Finally, he sighed and spoke. "It doesn't look good. You should've pled guilty. All your attorney has done is made the judge and everyone in that courtroom angry."

Knox didn't look him in the eyes. Instead, he stared at his hands, his fingers twitching with nervous energy. "Aunt Mary hired that lawyer. I figured she must've paid a bunch of money, so I just shut up and did what he told me," he murmured, his voice barely above a whisper.

Sheriff Price gave a small, almost imperceptible nod. "It'll be over with tomorrow," he said, his tone flat. He turned to leave but paused at the door. "Knox, I hope you know it's not personal. I'm just doing my job."

Knox nodded, but his mind was still clouded with uncertainty. "What's going to happen to me?" he asked, his voice cracking as the question tumbled out.

Price hesitated before answering, his eyes softening. "Can't tell you for certain. All I can say is... hope for the best but prepare for the worst."

With that, the sheriff left, his footsteps fading down the hall. Knox sat there in the silence that followed, his heart thumping loudly in his chest. He couldn't shake the feeling that the end was drawing near, but he wasn't sure if that meant freedom or the gallows.

As the sound of boots approached once again, Josiah Taylor appeared, his figure moving quickly down the dimly lit hallway. He was accompanied by a deputy, whose expression was just as stoic as ever.

"Good news, Knox!" Taylor's voice was bright, a stark contrast to the darkness in the cell.

The deputy opened the cell, and Taylor walked in with a grin on his face, his eyes gleaming with the hint of something hopeful. Knox, who had been slumping in his seat, looked up at him with cautious curiosity.

"I just talked to Melissa Scruggs," Taylor said, his tone low but full of excitement. "Her husband, Alan, is the foreman of the jury. Last year, John Whittemeyer sold her father a sick horse that died a few days later. Whittemeyer promised to give the money back but never did. Their whole family hates him!"

Knox's eyes widened slightly, the tiniest spark of hope igniting within him. "You saying that they're really gonna let me go free?" he asked, his voice tentative, unsure if he dared to believe what he was hearing.

Taylor's smile grew as he took a step closer to Knox. "I can't guarantee it, but I think you have a chance now! Worst case, life in prison…"

The weight that had been pressing on Knox's chest seemed to lighten, if only for a moment. He sat up straighter, his shoulders relaxing. A small, cautious hope began to flicker inside him.

Taylor straightened, giving Knox one last look of reassurance. "I'll be back in the morning," he said, turning to leave. "Is there anything you need?"

Knox shook his head, a small sense of relief settling in his bones. "No, sir."

As Taylor exited the cell, Knox remained sitting, still processing the words, the potential change in his fate. The door closed behind Taylor with a soft click, and for the first time in what felt like forever, Knox Martin allowed himself to believe that there might still be a chance for him—just maybe.

♦ ♦ ♦ ♦ ♦ ♦

The following morning, the courtroom was packed to the brim, a heavy silence settling over the room as the jury took their seats. The air felt thick with anticipation, every pair of eyes focused on the proceedings. Aunt Mary sat in the back, quietly knitting as she watched the room, her sharp gaze never straying from the action. Scott Singer, ever diligent, scribbled notes furiously, his eyes darting between the judge and the jury.

The doors to the courtroom opened with a soft creak as Judge Quarles entered, his presence commanding the room. A hush fell over the crowd as he made his way to the bench, his robe swishing lightly against the floor. He sat down and shuffled his papers, signaling the beginning of the day's proceedings.

"Mr. Norris, will you please open the court?" Judge Quarles said, his voice ringing with authority.

Deputy Norris stepped forward, his hand resting on the edge of the podium. "The honorable Criminal Court of Davidson County is now in session."

The jury slowly filed in, each man taking his seat with the solemnity of the task before them. The door closed softly behind them, and the air in the courtroom seemed to hold its breath.

"Mr. Norris, is everyone present? Call over this jury," Judge Quarles directed.

Deputy Norris stood, his voice calm as he called out each name. "Noah Price. John Brannon. William Hill. George Sweeney. George Clark. John Wilson. Walter Bush. Theodore Warren. Wade Cotton. John Jordan. James Creech. Alan Scruggs."

As each name was called, the corresponding juror raised his hand, acknowledging their presence. When Alan Scruggs' name was called, he stood, his eyes meeting Knox's with a brief flicker of empathy. Josiah Taylor, Knox's defense attorney, leaned over and gently urged Knox to stand as well. The young man did so, his face betraying little emotion, his expression stoic.

"We have," Alan Scruggs said, his voice steady.

Judge Quarles looked directly at the foreman. "What is your verdict, gentlemen?"

There was a brief pause before Alan Scruggs spoke again, his voice ringing through the quiet courtroom. "We find the defendant, Knox Martin, guilty of murder in the first degree."

The words hung in the air like a death knell. The sound of Aunt Mary's knitting needles came to an abrupt halt. Knox's shoulders sagged, the finality of the verdict sinking deep into his bones. The room seemed to tighten around him, every eye focused on him with a mix of judgment and expectation.

Judge Quarles turned toward the jury. "So say you all?"

One by one, each juror nodded in agreement, their voices a unanimous echo. "Yes."

Knox's heart raced in his chest, his breath shallow. He couldn't bring himself to look at anyone. He felt like a prisoner already, trapped in the suffocating certainty of the trial's outcome.

"But Mr. Taylor!" Knox's voice broke through the silence, his protest a last-ditch effort to hold on to something — anything — before the final blow came.

Judge Quarles raised his hand, his voice cutting through the room. "Now, now…" He brought the gavel down with a sharp crack, silencing Knox's protest in an instant.

"To the jury," Judge Quarles continued, his tone unyielding. "Thank you. You can now be discharged."

The jury filed out, the room growing quieter with each step they took. As the last of the jurors left the room, Judge Quarles turned his gaze to Knox. "Knox, have you anything to say why the sentence of the court should not be pronounced upon you?"

Knox swallowed hard, the words stuck in his throat. He didn't know what to say. He had no defense left, no way to undo what had already been done. He simply shook his head, his heart heavy with the inevitability of it all.

Judge Quarles stood, his voice filling the room with his authority. "Knox Martin, you have, after a fair and impartial trial, been convicted of the highest and most heinous offense known to the laws of Tennessee."

The judge's words rang in Knox's ears, each one a hammer driving the nail deeper into his fate. He wanted to close his eyes, to make it stop, but he couldn't.

"The jury which returned this verdict against you was impartial, honest, just, and intelligent," Judge

Quarles continued. "The court is satisfied with the verdict, and it must stand."

Knox looked helplessly toward Aunt Mary, who was now growing visibly angrier. Her expression was hard, and she seemed to seethe with frustration. For a moment, Knox thought she might leap up and storm the room.

"For this crime," Judge Quarles went on, his voice cold and unfeeling, "the law says you must die, and it now becomes my painful duty to pronounce its judgment. No earthly power can now aid you."

Knox's chest tightened, his breath quickening. He had thought it might come to this, but hearing it, hearing the cold finality of it, made it all the more real. His entire body seemed to sink under the weight of the words.

"Your only hope," the judge continued, "is in the all-abounding and saving grace of the crucified Redeemer. The court would most earnestly exhort you to address yourself to the Throne of Mercy and be prepared to meet your God."

The words felt like an echo, an attempt to provide some kind of solace, but it did little to ease Knox's mounting dread.

"It is therefore the judgment of this court that for the crime of murder in the first degree committed by you on the persons of John Whittemeyer and Emily Whittemeyer in this county on the 16th day of January, 1879…"

Knox's heart pounded in his chest, each word a painful reminder of the events that had led him here.

"By that verdict," Judge Quarles continued, "that you, Knox Martin, be taken from this courtroom to the jail of Davidson County and be delivered to the sheriff, who will keep you safely and securely confined in said jail until the 28th day of March, 1879, when, upon a gallows previously erected by him, within one mile of this courthouse, he will between the hours of ten o'clock a.m. and two o'clock p.m. hang you by the neck until you are dead. May God have mercy on your soul."

The courtroom was silent, the air thick with tension and sorrow. Aunt Mary stood abruptly, her chair scraping against the floor, the sound sharp and jarring in the stillness.

"This verdict is not just!" she shouted, her voice filled with fury and desperation. She stormed out of the courtroom, her feet heavy against the floor as she left in a flurry of rage.

Judge Quarles glared after her, his face tight with irritation. He turned back to the courtroom, his gaze fixed on Knox.

"Mr. Norris," Judge Quarles barked, his voice firm. "Will you please take the prisoner to jail?"

Deputy Norris stepped forward, his expression grim as he approached Knox.

"Come with me," he said flatly.

Knox stood, his legs shaky beneath him. He was led through a side door, the cold hallway stretching out before him. He felt like a shadow of himself, the reality of the situation sinking in with each step.

As Knox left the courtroom, he saw a distinguished looking man approach Sheriff Price.

"Sheriff, I'm Doctor Randall Summers. Is it possible to speak with the prisoner?" the doctor asked, his voice calm but carrying a sense of urgency.

Sheriff Price looked at the doctor with a confused expression. "What do you want with him?"

Dr. Summers didn't hesitate. "There have been some tremendous advances in science in the past few years."

Price raised an eyebrow, the strange request not sitting well with him. "I can't stop anyone from coming by the jail and visiting a prisoner, but it's been a rough morning. You're welcome to stop by, just give him a day or two."

"Of course, Sheriff. I understand completely," Dr. Summers said, offering a polite nod before turning to leave.

# The Redeemer

The small cell was quiet, save for the occasional clink of metal from the distant sound of guards' boots echoing down the hall. Knox sat on his cot, the thin mattress uncomfortable beneath him, but the physical discomfort was nothing compared to the mental weight he carried. The looming sentence, the endless questions about his fate—it was all too much to bear. His eyes drifted to the door when he saw Sheriff Price walking down the hall toward him. The sheriff's footsteps echoed louder with each step.

"Sheriff!" Knox called out softly.

Price paused, looking over at him before making his way to the cell door.

"Can I ask you something?"

Price stopped, standing before him. His expression softened, but only slightly, as he nodded. "Sure."

"What'd you think about what the judge said today?" Knox asked, his words coming out almost too quickly.

Price's eyebrows crinkled for a moment, clearly a little taken aback by the question. He scratched his head, then let out a long breath. "Well, to be honest, today went about as I expected it to. You have the right to appeal the verdict if you think it wasn't just."

Knox shook his head, the faintest trace of a bitter smile crossing his face. "No, no. I meant about the Redeemer stuff, and meeting God. What's going to happen to me after I'm hanged?"

There was a brief, uncomfortable pause. Price didn't immediately respond, and when he did, his voice held an edge of unease, as if he didn't quite know how to comfort the young man. "Son, I grew up in the church, but I'm the last person you'd want to get religious advice from." He shifted uncomfortably on his feet. "If you want to talk with someone, I can get a preacher to come by to talk with you. He'll be better equipped to answer any questions you might have about all that stuff."

Knox nodded slowly, digesting the sheriff's words. "Okay," he murmured, his voice a mix of uncertainty and resignation.

"It's been a long day," Price continued, the exhaustion clear in his tone. "Get some sleep."

With one final glance, Price turned and walked back down the hall, his footsteps echoing in the silence that remained.

♦ ♦ ♦ ♦ ♦ ♦

The morning came too soon, its light creeping in through the narrow window of Knox's cell. He lay there, eyes closed, but sleep was a stranger. The looming date on the scaffold hung over him like a thick fog.

When the door to the cell finally creaked open, Knox blinked, struggling to push himself upright. Josiah Taylor stood at the entrance, accompanied by Deputy Norris.

"Good morning, Knox," Taylor said, his voice cheerful but slightly forced. "Were you able to get any sleep?"

Knox rubbed his face with his hands, trying to clear the haze of exhaustion. "Didn't sleep too much. Got a lot on my mind."

Taylor looked at him sympathetically but quickly

moved to the subject at hand. "I'm sorry. I thought we had a chance at getting life in prison. Have you thought about appealing to the Supreme Court? Aunt Mary said she would support you if you wanted to file a motion."

Knox's lips tightened. He had thought about it, but the thought of dragging everything out, only to face the same inevitable end, seemed pointless. "We both know how this all ends," he replied, his tone flat. "Dragging it out ain't gonna change things. I don't want to sit in here for a year waiting for another judge to tell me I'm gonna be executed."

Visibly unsettled by Knox's resolve, Taylor hesitated for a moment. "Perhaps I could appeal to the governor. Governor Marks might have some compassion."

Knox chuckled, though it was a hollow sound. "He is a good man," he said, his voice distant. "I talked to him already. Had breakfast in the governor's mansion a few days ago."

Taylor's eyebrows shot up in surprise. "What?"

"The sheriff and I dropped by to see him." Knox shrugged slightly.

Taylor looked skeptical. "Well, he might commute the sentence. If he were to act, you'd be able to spend the rest of your life in prison."

Knox shook his head, and smiled slightly, though it didn't quite reach his eyes. "Life in prison ain't living. The judge gave me a date on the gallows. I'd rather just get it over with."

Before Taylor could respond, Nelson Merry, an older African American pastor, appeared at the cell door with Deputy Norris.

"Knox," Deputy Norris said, his voice soft but firm,

"This is Reverend Merry from the Baptist Church. Sheriff Price told me that you wanted to meet with him."

Taylor gave a quick glance toward Knox, still unsure, but he didn't push the subject further. "Knox, are you sure you don't want to appeal the conviction?" Taylor pressed, his voice laced with concern. "I think we could get a new trial. You have that right."

Knox shook his head again, a mix of resignation and weariness filling him. "No, sir. It's not worth the fight. Thank you."

He extended his hand to shake Taylor's, who nodded solemnly before turning and leaving.

As Taylor disappeared down the hallway, Reverend Merry stepped forward, offering a gentle smile. "Good morning, son. I'm Nelson Merry. I understand you have some questions for me. I'd be happy to talk with you."

Knox swallowed hard. He nodded slowly, gesturing for the pastor to sit. "Yes. A lot has been on my mind lately. I've done some awful things. The judge was talking about God and the Throne of Mercy yesterday. Can you tell me about the Redeemer?"

Reverend Merry lowered himself to sit beside Knox on the edge of the cot, his hands carefully folding the Bible in his lap. "I know you've done something terrible, but the Lord still loves you," the pastor said gently. "You can still be forgiven. Let me show you something."

With that, Reverend Merry opened the Bible, his fingers tracing the pages slowly. Knox leaned in, his curiosity piqued.

"It says here in the First Letter of John, 'If we confess our sins, He is faithful and just to forgive us our sins, and to cleanse us from all unrighteousness.'

Merry looked him in the eye. "Do you know what that means, son? God still loves you. He will forgive you."

Knox tilted his head, intrigued. "Tell me more, Reverend."

Reverend Merry flipped through the Bible, showing him other scriptures. Knox listened intently, feeling something stir inside him that he hadn't felt in a long time—hope.

◆ ◆ ◆ ◆ ◆ ◆

Later that afternoon, the hallway was quiet except for the soft echoes of footsteps on the stone floor. Reverend Merry walked slowly down the corridor, his gaze focused ahead, deep in thought. He was nearly at the end when he saw Sheriff Price approaching.

"Hello, Reverend," the sheriff greeted with a nod. Merry paused and smiled warmly. "Sheriff, it's nice to see you."

Price returned the smile, but there was a certain heaviness in his eyes as he looked at the pastor. "How is he?"

Reverend Merry took a deep breath, his expression growing serious. "He's alright, considering the circumstances. We spent a lot of time talking about the Bible. That poor boy has never read it. He wasn't raised properly. All his life, he grew up with his momma practicing some kind of voodoo around him. He's never heard the Word of God."

Sheriff Price nodded, his face a mix of concern and empathy. He shook his head. "I hope you can give him some comfort and some peace in his last few days."

Reverend Merry's eyes softened as he talked. "There's hope for him. He did an awful thing on that farm, but he can still be born again. There's still time."

Sheriff Price gave a small, understanding nod. "You are a good man."

As Price turned to leave, he clapped Reverend Merry gently on the back. Merry watched him walk away, the sheriff's words echoed in his mind as he continued down the hallway, his thoughts with the troubled young man locked behind bars.

♦ ♦ ♦ ♦ ♦ ♦

After the sun went down, the jail was eerily quiet. Knox sat in his cell, the dim light from a candle casting shadows against the stone walls. He leaned back, a cigar between his fingers, the smoke swirling around him as he read the Bible. The words were unfamiliar, but there was a sense of peace in them, a strange comfort he hadn't expected to find.

His thoughts were interrupted by the sound of footsteps coming down the hall, slow but deliberate. Sheriff Price appeared in front of the cell, accompanied by a deputy. He looked down at Knox, his expression serious but not unkind.

"Mind if I join you for a few minutes?" Price asked.

Knox looked up from his Bible, a faint smile crossing his face. "No sir. C'mon in."

The deputy unlocked the door, and Price entered, sitting down next to Knox on the cot.

"I want you to be comfortable here the next few days," Price said, his tone softer now. "Is there anything I can get you or do for you?"

Knox leaned back, blowing out a puff of smoke before answering. "Nah, sheriff. Everybody's been real nice. Reverend Merry came by today. He gave me a Bible, and we talked for a long time. He thinks I should get baptized. What do you think?"

Price was quiet for a moment, the question clearly weighing on him. He looked at Knox, his gaze thoughtful. "Well, that's a decision only you can make, Knox," he said slowly. "It's not something anyone else can decide for you."

Knox nodded, but there was a trace of uncertainty in his eyes. He looked down at the deck of cards in his hands, fidgeting with the edges.

Price stood up, signaling for the deputy to unlock the door. "It's been a long day," he said, stretching his legs. "I'd better get over to the courthouse. I need to check the docket for tomorrow."

"Hey, Sheriff," Knox called, his voice lightening a little. "The preacher gave me a deck of cards, but I ain't got no one to play with." He held up the deck, a small, half-hearted grin on his face. "You want to play bluff?"

Price smiled, shaking his head with a chuckle. "I really need to get over there, but I suppose I have a few minutes. What are we playing for?"

Price raised an eyebrow, his grin widening. "I'd hate to take all your cigars."

The two men shared a laugh as Price waved the deputy off, signaling him to leave the cell. The deputy hesitated for a moment, but then stepped out, leaving the two men alone.

Knox shuffled the cards with practiced hands, the noise of the cards hitting one another the only sound in the room. Price sat back down, a genuine smile on his face as he prepared for a game that, despite the gravity of the situation, seemed to lighten the air in the small, dimly lit cell.

# Galvanism

The prison yard was quiet, the spring sun warming the air, as Knox sat along the wall with a few other prisoners. They were enjoying the rare moment of calm, basking in the nice weather. Deputy Peter Pirtle, a jovial man in his fifties with a tall frame, pulled up in a horse-drawn wagon, the heavy clatter of the wheels echoing through the yard as he approached.

"Hey, boys," Pirtle called out, a broad smile on his face. "Need y'all to help me unload this over in that clearing in the yard."

The prisoners stood up, stretching and grumbling as they made their way over to the wagon. They hadn't been expecting to work today, but the sight of the lumber piled high on the cart was enough to get them moving. Knox watched as they started to unload, feeling a sense of unease settle in his stomach. He couldn't help but ask.

"What y'all gonna build?"

There was a brief hesitation from Pirtle, who shifted uncomfortably in the seat of the wagon. "Uh, this is for you," he finally said, his tone uncharacteristically somber. "We have to have the gallows built by the end of the week so the sheriff can inspect it. We are going to build part of it back here and then carry it to the site."

The words hit Knox like a punch to the gut. He froze for a moment, unsure of what to say, his breath catching in his throat. He'd known the day was coming, but hearing it spoken so plainly made it all feel real in a way he wasn't prepared for. His mouth went dry, and he could only stand there in silence, the sounds of the other prisoners resuming work around him fading into the background.

"Knox!" a voice called out sharply.

Deputy Norris was walking toward him, a figure standing just behind him. As they came closer, Knox noticed the gentleman.

"Knox," Deputy Norris said, his voice gentler now, "this is Dr. Summers. He's a professor over at the University of Nashville. He asked if he could speak to you."

Dr. Randall Summers stepped forward and extended his hand. "Mr. Martin, if you have a moment, I'd like to talk with you about an idea I have."

Knox shrugged. "As long as the deputies don't mind, I have all the time in the world, sir."

Summers grinned, a wide, eager smile that made Knox feel slightly uneasy. Deputy Norris nodded and gave them both some space. The conversation shifted quickly, and Dr. Summers seemed intent on keeping Knox's attention.

"Do you know what galvanism is?" Summers asked, his voice smooth and calm.

Knox blinked, clearly confused. "Galvanism?" he repeated, trying to make sense of the word. "I ain't heard of it."

Summers nodded, clearly pleased that he had piqued Knox's curiosity. "Are you familiar with the book *Frankenstein*?" he asked, his tone softening, though there was still an excitement in his eyes.

"I ain't never read it," Knox replied, shifting on his feet, "but I heard it's about a monster."

"Indeed," Summers said, "and no. In the book, Dr. Victor Frankenstein uses electric current to give life to his creature."

Knox's brow furrowed in confusion as Summers went on. "Knox, there have been some exciting developments and breakthroughs in the world of science that I never thought possible. There is a doctor in Maryland who has successfully revived a dead frog using a galvanized battery."

Knox's eyes widened. Deputy Norris was equally impressed, his mouth slightly agape.

"I have recently acquired the elements needed to create a battery," Summers continued, his voice lowering slightly, as though he were about to share a secret. "I'm hoping to conduct some experiments of my own. Would you be willing to donate your remains to me after the execution?"

Knox froze. The words seemed to hang in the air like smoke, hazy and unsettling. He couldn't quite grasp what Summers was suggesting.

"I would compensate you handsomely, of course," Summers added quickly, as if to reassure him. "One hundred dollars, if you agree to have your body turned over to me after your execution."

Knox didn't know what to think. His mind raced, and he felt as though the world around him was spinning. This was a lot to process, especially with everything that had already happened.

"Would you mind if I took a day or so to think it over?" Knox asked, his voice steady despite the confusion flooding his mind.

Summers smiled broadly. "Yes, of course. Take all the time you need."

Knox shook the man's hand. As Summers turned to leave, Deputy Norris spoke up.

"You don't have much to lose," he said, his tone

almost conversational. "That is a substantial amount of money. You could eat like a king for your last few days."

Knox looked over at him, considering the suggestion. "What would you do?" he asked, the question coming out before he could stop it.

Deputy Norris hesitated, his face momentarily softening. "I'm married, and my family could probably use the money," he admitted. "You could send it back to your family. I'm sure it would help them."

Knox thought about it for a long moment. It was hard to deny that the money could be useful, especially for his family back home in Alabama.

"I reckon it would," Knox replied quietly.

As he pondered his decision, Deputy Norris led him back to the wagon, where the other prisoners were finishing up their work with the lumber. The task at hand seemed insignificant compared to what was unfolding, but the rest of the day had a heaviness to it that wouldn't leave Knox's mind.

# Amazing Grace

Later that evening, the dim light of the cell barely illuminated the pages of the Bible Knox was reading. He sat on the edge of the cot, his legs crossed beneath him, engrossed in the verses. The quiet of the night was broken by the sound of footsteps approaching. Sheriff Price arrived with a deputy, who unlocked the cell as he stepped aside.

"What are you reading?" Price asked, his voice calm but tinged with curiosity.

Knox looked up from the Bible. "Psalms," he said. "It's very interesting. Gives me a lot of hope."

"Well, that's good," Price replied sincerely. "I'm sure you can use all the hope you can get right now."

Knox nodded, his face clouded with thought. "Growing up, I never read the Bible. My granddaddy had one, but I'm not even sure he could read it. Momma never took me to church. She'd pray sometimes, but it wasn't to the Lord." He sighed deeply, looking down at the pages before him. "That's what got me in this mess."

Price didn't reply immediately. He could see the regret in the young man's eyes, the burden of his past weighing on him more than the physical confinement of the cell.

"Well," Price said after a beat, "you don't have much time left. I'm glad to see that you're trying to get yourself right with the Lord."

Knox's face softened slightly, a sense of calm settling over him. "I talked to Reverend Merry again today. I'm gonna get baptized tomorrow."

"That's great, Knox," Price replied, offering a faint smile.

Knox hesitated, then spoke with a quieter urgency. "Would you like to come?"

Price looked at him, conflicted. His lips parted as though he were about to speak, but then he paused, considering his words. "I don't know," he said finally. "I think I'm due in court tomorrow and Wednesday."

The disappointment was clear on Knox's face, and Price could see it, his heart twinging with empathy. "Tell you what," Price said, his voice firm with determination, "let me see if I can move some things around."

Knox's eyes brightened slightly at the prospect. "Thank you," he said, his voice laced with genuine gratitude.

There was a long pause as Knox looked down at the Bible. He seemed to be gathering his thoughts. "I wanted to ask you about something," he began, his voice hesitating. "A doctor stopped by today and offered me a lot of money to give them my body after I was hanged."

Price's expression darkened a little, his eyes narrowing. "Yeah, I spoke to him about it the other day." Knox continued, his tone more steady now. "I think I'm going to do it, but only if you'll help me with something." He gave Price a sidelong glance.

Price raised an eyebrow, clearly intrigued. "What's that?"

Knox's voice dropped a little, the weight of what he was about to say sinking in. "The doctor told me he'd give me one hundred dollars. If I gave you the money, would you take it to John Whittemeyer's brother-in-law? I'd like for him to have it so he can provide for little Johnny."

Sheriff Price stood still for a moment, the request taking him by surprise. His face softened, touched by the gesture. "Of course," he said quietly. "I'd be happy to do that."

"Thank you," Knox replied, his voice thick with emotion.

There was an awkward silence that followed as Knox reflected on the choices he'd made. He glanced down at the floor, trying to collect his thoughts before speaking again.

"One more thing," he said, his voice trembling slightly. "If that doctor manages to bring me back to life, will y'all have to hang me again?"

Price froze, caught off guard by the question. His face softened, and he let out a small chuckle. "I don't think they'll be able to resurrect you, Knox. But if they do... oh man, those boys over at the capitol will be up all night sorting it out." He laughed again, the sound dry but genuine.

Knox managed a nervous smile, the tension in his chest easing just a little.

Price's tone shifted as he glanced at the deck of cards on the small table in front of Knox. "The reason I stopped by tonight," he said, shifting the conversation, "is I need all my nickels and pennies back you got me for."

Knox raised an eyebrow, a grin tugging at the corner of his mouth. "You want me to deal you in?"

Price smiled in return, his eyes lighting up with a familiar spark. "I'm getting all my money back, and I'm taking your stash of cigars!"

Knox chuckled as he shuffled the deck of cards, the motion fluid and practiced. "After I take all your money," he said with a teasing grin, "I'm going to get that badge!"

Price shook his head, trying not to laugh.

As the two men settled in, the looming execution faded into the background, replaced by the lighthearted banter of two men sharing a moment of rare camaraderie in a place where moments of kindness were hard to come by.

♦ ♦ ♦ ♦ ♦ ♦

An hour later, Sheriff Price entered the jail office, his head shaking slightly as he walked in. Deputy Norris looked up from his desk, sensing that something was off.

"I used to think I knew how to play cards," Price said with a soft chuckle. "Every time I went to the Silver Dollar, I left with everybody's money. But that kid beats me just about every time."

Norris chuckled, clearly amused by the sheriff's admission. "Seems like you and him are pals."

Price nodded, but his expression softened, distant. "He reminds me of my nephew, Carl."

"I don't think I ever met him," Norris said, setting his pen down, curious.

"No," Price replied, his voice quieter now. "After my brother died about ten years ago, his wife moved back to Virginia to be closer to her mother. Carl didn't have a daddy or anyone to show him how to be a man. I wrote him and took the train to see him a few times, but they were just so far away."

Price paused for a moment, lost in the memory. "When Carl got a little older, he started running with a rough bunch. One day, he got caught helping some guys robbing a bank. They're pretty strict about that kind of thing over in the Commonwealth."

He paused again, the words catching in his throat. "They hanged him for it. He was just a kid. Knox is just like him, grew up a slave with no father, and the only people he had were two old bats who believed in voodoo. He never had a shot."

Deputy Norris listened in silence.

"You going to be ok up there on the gallows?" Norris asked quietly.

Price didn't answer immediately. He looked down at the floor, lost in thought for a moment before speaking again. "Yeah."

"If you need me to do it..." Norris offered hesitantly.

Price shot him a sharp look. "No," he replied firmly. "I'm not having anyone else do it."

Norris was quiet for a moment, the tension hanging in the air between them. The silence between them grew, but neither man spoke.

◆ ◆ ◆ ◆ ◆ ◆

Reverend Merry, Knox, and Sheriff Price stepped into the jail yard, the morning sun beginning to rise over the jail. They approached a large trough filled with water, its surface still in the early light.

Knox looked at the water warily and turned to Price. "You reckon that water is cold?"

Price stuck his hand into the trough, then pulled it back quickly with a laugh. "It ain't warm!"

A handful of curious inmates gathered around,

eyeing the scene with interest. Reverend Merry greeted them with a nod, his face radiating calm.

"Gentlemen," he began, his voice carrying, "today is a special day. Brother Knox is going to be baptized. Would you care to join us in singing *Amazing Grace*?"

The reverend began to sing, his voice steady and filled with purpose. Slowly, the other inmates joined in, their voices creating a rough but heartfelt chorus. The song echoed through the yard, creating a brief moment of shared unity among the men.

When the final notes of the song faded, Reverend Merry helped Knox into the trough. Knox stepped in, then immediately climbed back out, shivering.

"Sheriff, you were right," Knox said, his teeth chattering. "It's freezing!"

Laughter broke out from the small crowd of onlookers. Knox hesitated but then climbed back in, sitting down carefully in the cold water. Reverend Merry placed his hands gently on Knox's back and head.

"Knox Martin," he said, his tone serious but kind, "have you received Jesus Christ as your Lord and Savior?"

"Yes sir," Knox replied, his voice clear but soft.

"Will you obey and serve Him for the rest of your life?"

"Yes sir."

"Because you've professed your faith in the Lord, I baptize you in the name of the Father, Son, and Holy Spirit."

With that, he carefully lowered Knox backward into the water. The coldness of the water didn't seem to faze him now. When Knox rose from the water, he suddenly pulled Reverend Merry into a bear hug, causing the small crowd to laugh politely.

"Sorry, Reverend," Knox said, his voice thick with emotion.

Reverend Merry chuckled, wiping water from his face. "It's okay, son. But you're right. That water is mighty cold!"

Sheriff Price handed Knox a towel, smiling as he watched the scene unfold. The simple act of baptism, in the midst of everything, seemed to offer a brief respite from the inevitable fate awaiting Knox. The crowd began to disperse, leaving the three of them alone, but the warmth of the moment lingered in the cool morning air.

Still dripping wet from the baptism, Knox walked back to his cell, flanked by Sheriff Price and Reverend Merry. The chill from the water clung to him as he moved, his footsteps echoing in the quiet prison hallway. As they approached the corner, Deputy Pirtle turned, noticing them.

"Hey, your aunt is here to see you," he said, glancing at Knox with a hint of concern in his eyes.

Before Knox could react, Aunt Mary appeared around the corner. Her eyes flicked over to them, her smile quickly fading as she took in the sight of Knox, still wet, standing between the sheriff and the reverend. Knox's heart skipped a beat at the sight of her, a mix of relief and unease swirling within him.

"Aunt Mary!" he called, his voice filled with hope, but the joy of seeing her quickly faded as he took in her stern expression.

"What is all this?" she demanded, her voice sharp.

Sheriff Price stepped forward, offering a greeting. "Good morning, ma'am."

But Aunt Mary paid him no mind, brushing past

him with a swiftness that left the lawman standing there, momentarily speechless. Her attention was fixed solely on Reverend Merry, her gaze cold and searching, her posture rigid with indignation.

The reverend was caught off-guard, clearly surprised by the woman's sudden presence and fury. He stammered for a moment before Knox spoke up, attempting to explain.

"This is Reverend Merry from the Baptist Church. He just baptized me," Knox said, his voice unsure but earnest.

Aunt Mary's fury only deepened. "Baptized?" she repeated, her voice thick with disbelief.

Without warning, she slapped Knox across the face, the sting sharp and immediate. He recoiled, his face burning with the suddenness of the blow. Aunt Mary turned back to Reverend Merry, her anger palpable.

"Why you been telling the boy these lies?" she demanded, her voice rising with fury. "There is only Bondye!"

Still trying to maintain his composure, Reverend Merry struggled to respond but found himself faltering under Aunt Mary's harsh gaze. She ignored him completely, her attention once again fixed on Knox.

"You are a fool!" she spat at him, her voice filled with contempt.

The hallway fell silent as all eyes turned toward Aunt Mary. Her words hung in the air. Without another word, she turned and slowly hobbled away, her footsteps echoing in the silence she left behind.

Knox stood there, his hand still raised to his stinging cheek, a deep sadness settling in his chest. The words of Aunt Mary lingered, the sting of her rejection sharper than any physical pain. He watched her go, feeling the blunt of her anger as the others in the hallway resumed their work. The atmosphere of that previously joyful morning had shifted. Everything felt colder, heavier.

♦ ♦ ♦ ♦ ♦ ♦

After the baptism, Price and Merry led Knox back to his cell. Merry could see the turmoil on Knox's face, so he put a comforting arm around his shoulders. "Don't pay her no mind," he said softly, giving Knox a big hug. "I love you, brother. I'm so proud of you."

Still troubled, Knox managed a faint smile. Price shook his hand, offering a quiet, reassuring squeeze.

"You could still do a lot of good work for His Kingdom, Knox. Maybe the governor could do something," Price said, his voice steady with quiet hope.

Knox shook his head. "I don't think so."

Merry leaned in, his tone firm but hopeful. "But if he could grant you life in prison, you could minister to those who need to hear His word."

Knox's eyes flickered with interest. "Well, if that is what the Lord wants me to do, I'd do it."

Merry smiled brightly. "I'm going to pray about it. If it's God's will, He'll see it through."

With that, the three of them turned to leave, walking down the corridor together.

Merry spoke up again, his voice laced with a hint of hope. "Do you think if I went and spoke to the governor, he'd commute his sentence? Knox should be punished for what he's done, but with life in prison, he could make a difference."

Price shook his head slowly, a deep sigh escaping him. "No, sir," he replied. "I agree. He's been a model prisoner, and he could be a positive influence on others. But the governor is familiar with his case. He told me himself that the jury would decide his fate. You're welcome to go meet with him, but I already know what he's going to say."

Merry paused, his shoulders heavy with disappointment.

"I still got to try."

He patted Price on the back and walked down the hall.

◆ ◆ ◆ ◆ ◆ ◆

A few hours later, Knox heard a noise from outside his cell. He looked out the small window and saw prisoners loading pieces of the scaffold into a wagon. The sight made his stomach tighten. The inevitable was drawing closer.

As he turned away from the window, he saw Sheriff Price approaching, accompanied by a deputy. The deputy unlocked the door and let Price inside.

"I brought you something," Price said, his voice carrying a hint of something softer than usual.

Price handed Knox a package wrapped in twine. Knox took it and untied the knot. Inside, he found a neatly folded suit and a white dress shirt. He looked up, his expression mixed with surprise and gratitude.

"I don't want you up on that scaffold looking like an inmate," Price said quietly. "You should be wearing this."

Knox was touched, his hand shaking slightly as he

reached out to shake Price's hand. Then, holding the suit up to get a better look, he said, "I don't know what to say, sheriff. It's very nice."

Price grew eerily quiet, his eyes shifting as if he wanted to say something but couldn't find the words.

"Sheriff?" Knox asked, breaking the stillness.

Price cleared his throat, his expression tightening. "I want you to know that I'll be the one who cuts the rope that drops the trap door tomorrow. I don't like it, but it's part of the job. I knew it was part of my duties when I got elected."

Knox stood and placed a hand on Price's shoulder, his touch firm and reassuring. "It's gonna be ok. You got a job to do."

Price's face softened for a moment. He seemed to carry a tinge of guilt he couldn't quite shake.

"If you'd like," Price said after a beat, his voice quieter, "I can arrange to have you photographed in the suit, and we can send it to your mother in Alabama."

Knox's eyes brightened slightly, the idea comforting him. "That would be nice. I ain't never had nobody take my picture before."

As if on instinct, Knox reached under his pillow and pulled out an envelope. "That doctor came calling a few hours ago," he said. "Please make sure this gets in the hands of Little Johnny's uncle."

Price took the envelope from Knox and tucked it into his pocket. "You can count on it."

A small smile crept across Price's face as he pulled the envelope back out. "Grab them cards. I got some more money to play with!"

Knox chuckled softly. As Price sat down on the cot, shuffling the cards, Knox joined him. The two of them sat together in silence for a moment, the mundane task of playing cards offering a brief reprieve from the storm of emotions they both carried.

◆ ◆ ◆ ◆ ◆ ◆

The halls of the capitol were dimly lit as the sun began to set. Reverend Merry walked slowly down the corridor, his footsteps echoing softly in the quiet space.

At the end of the hall, the governor's office door was slightly ajar, and inside, voices could be heard murmuring in quiet conversation. Merry approached the receptionist at her desk, a woman in her late forties who looked up as he came near.

"Good evening, sir. Can I help you?" she asked politely.

"Hello, I'm Nelson Merry. I was hoping to speak with the governor, ma'am," Merry replied, his voice steady but his heart racing in anticipation.

The secretary hesitated, glancing at the clock on the wall. "The governor is in a meeting at the moment, Reverend. Would you like to sit and wait?"

"I'd be most appreciative," Merry said, offering a polite smile.

Merry walked over to a bench along the wall, settling into the seat as the sound of murmured voices continued from the office. He folded his hands in his lap, his mind preoccupied with thoughts of Knox, of the future he could have if only the governor would listen.

A few minutes passed before the door to the governor's office opened. Governor Marks stepped out, followed by an aide who handed him a few papers. As soon as the door swung open, Merry stood and moved quickly toward the governor.

"Governor, good evening," Merry said. He extended his hand, offering a smile, though it was tinged with the nerves of the moment.

The governor raised an eyebrow, clearly caught off guard by the unexpected visitor. He shook Merry's hand, his expression polite but distant. "Good evening, sir. Can I help you?"

"I'm Nelson Merry from the First Baptist Church," Merry replied, clearing his throat as he continued. "I was hoping we could speak about Knox Martin, the young man who's set to be executed."

The governor's eyebrows wrinkled at the mention of Knox's name, but he said nothing. Merry pressed on, his voice becoming more urgent.

"He's been baptized, born again. He's found redemption. And I believe, Governor, that if you were to commute his sentence, he could serve as a light for other troubled young men. He could really make a difference."

The governor's eyes narrowed slightly. He paused, clearly processing the words. "I've met Knox," he said flatly. "I'm familiar with his case. But in a situation like his — double murder, the jury's decision was clear. I can't step in."

Merry's shoulders sagged with disappointment. "So, you're saying there's nothing that can be done?"

"I'm afraid not," the governor replied. "I understand your desire to help him, but he admitted to killing that couple over in Bell's Bend. The sentence must be carried out."

Merry hesitated, his heart sinking in his chest. He'd hoped, against reason, that the governor might show mercy. But now, faced with the reality of the situation, he could only nod.

"I understand," Merry said softly, his voice thick with emotion. He held out his hand one last time. "I just wanted to ask, and I'll continue praying that you reconsider. Thank you for your time, Governor."

The governor gave him a polite nod but said nothing more, his attention already drifting to other matters.

Merry turned and walked out of the capitol, there was nothing he could do to save Knox.

# "I'm a Hansome Fella"

The morning of the execution had arrived. Sheriff Price awoke with a groan, glancing at his pocket watch on the nightstand. The time seemed to crawl as he slowly climbed out of bed, his body heavy with the weight of the day ahead. He walked to the bureau, pulling out his uniform with mechanical precision. The fabric of his uniform felt familiar as he put it on, each movement slow and methodical.

As he stepped out into the cool morning air, a boy around the corner shouted the morning's headline. "Bell's Bend Killer to be Executed Today!" he hollered, holding up a stack of newspapers for sale. A small crowd of people rushed over, digging coins from their pockets to buy a copy. Price shook his head as he passed, the bustle of the town doing little to lift his spirits.

When he reached the jail, a deputy opened the door, granting him access to the courtyard. There, Reverend Merry sat on a bench, Bible in hand, quietly ministering to two inmates.

"Good morning, Sheriff," Merry called out with a gentle nod.

Price gave a gruff smile. The weight of the day's proceedings pressed on him, heavy and suffocating. Merry excused himself from the prisoners and fell into step beside Price as they walked.

"I spoke to the governor last night," Merry said hesitantly.

Price gave him a side glance.

Merry shook his head slightly.

"Figured as much," Price replied flatly.

"We'll be leaving here soon," Price added, pausing for a moment. "Did you want to ride out to the creek with us?"

Merry hesitated, then nodded. "Yes, sir. If it's not too much trouble."

Price gave a small nod before continuing on his way.

Just as he was about to reach the door, Merry's voice stopped him. "I want you to know I've been praying for you," he said quietly. "I know today isn't going to be easy. I don't envy the position you're in."

Price wasn't expecting that. The words caught him off guard, and for a brief moment, he faltered. He turned to look at Merry, his gruffness momentarily softened. "Thank you," he muttered, before continuing toward the door.

As he approached, Deputy Pirtle stood ready to open it for him. Price nodded in acknowledgment as Pirtle swung the door open, and the sheriff walked through, his thoughts heavy with the day that loomed ahead.

◆ ◆ ◆ ◆ ◆ ◆

Inside the jail, tension hung in the air, thick and suffocating. Deputy Norris approached Knox's cell, his footsteps echoing down the quiet hall.

"What would you like for breakfast?" Norris asked, his voice steady but carrying an undercurrent of unease.

"I'm not too hungry," Knox replied softly. "Could I get some eggs? Some toast would be nice if you have it."

Norris nodded. "I'm sure we can round some up for you. Anything else?"

"No sir."

Just then, Dr. Summers appeared at the cell door. "How are you feeling?" he asked, his tone clinical but compassionate.

"Not too good," Knox answered, shaking his head. "I'm a little jumpy. Couldn't really sleep last night."

"That's to be expected," Dr. Summers said, taking Knox's pulse. He frowned slightly, then turned to Norris. "Deputy, is it possible to get a bottle of wine in the jail? It might help him calm down. His heart is racing. He might have a heart attack before we get him to the gallows."

Norris snickered, clearly amused by the suggestion. "We don't have any in here, but I bet I can get you some. I'll go check on it." He walked off, leaving Knox and Dr. Summers alone.

Knox glanced down the hallway, making sure no one was nearby before he spoke. "I need a favor," he said.

Dr. Summers looked at him with a raised eyebrow, his demeanor cautious. "Um, what is it?"

"When this is all over," Knox said, his words tentative but earnest, "and you somehow manage to bring me back to life, can you help me get back home to my family in Alabama?"

Dr. Summers hesitated, then sighed softly. "Knox, according to the medical journals I've been reading, only a small amount of animals and livestock have been brought back, and only for a short time. I'm not sure my battery is powerful enough to fully revive you permanently. I don't want you to get your hopes up."

Knox's expression remained steady, but his voice softened with resolve. "Ok, well promise me this; no matter how it goes, you keep the findings to yourself. And if you do resurrect me, please help get me back home to Alabama. If I stay here, I have a feeling they're gonna want to hang me again."

"You have my word," Dr. Summers said, giving Knox a firm handshake.

As they finished their conversation, Deputy Norris returned, holding a bottle of wine in one hand and a plate of toast and eggs in the other. Jay Chapdelaine, a friendly photographer with a chatty disposition, trailed behind him.

"Here's that wine you were asking for," Norris said, handing Knox the wine and plate through the bars.

Knox picked at the eggs, barely tasting them, before he lifted the bottle of wine to his lips and took a long, hard swig. Dr. Summers watched him, then quickly intervened.

"Easy," he warned. "I'm sure the deputy doesn't want to carry you up that scaffold."

Knox chuckled and set the wine down, a wry smile tugging at his lips.

"Mr. Chapdelaine, the photographer is here," Norris said, stepping aside to let the photographer approach. "The sheriff said you requested to be photographed in your suit."

Knox nodded, his tone polite but weary. "Yes, sir. May I have a moment to get dressed?"

Deputy Norris opened the cell door, stepping back to allow Dr. Summers to leave. Knox quickly got dressed, sliding into his new suit with a sense of disbelief. He looked down at his arms, unable to fathom the fine jacket he now wore.

Norris led him down the hallway, his footsteps purposeful and steady. As they passed, a few of the other inmates, still locked behind their bars, let out catcalls and crude remarks about the dapper prisoner. Clearly aware of the attention, Knox flashed a playful smile. He straightened his posture, his movements taking on a theatrical flair as he strutted into the small meeting room where the photographer awaited.

Knox and Deputy Norris entered the small room. The photographer's bulky camera rested on a large tripod, with various pieces of equipment and vials of chemicals scattered across a nearby table.

"Good morning," Chapdelaine greeted, his eyes scanning Knox's attire. "You look very nice. Would you mind standing over here, directly in front of the camera?"

Knox nodded and moved into position, standing still as instructed.

"I've got everything set up," Chapdelaine continued, adjusting the equipment with meticulous care. "All I ask is that you remain perfectly still until I tell you to move."

Knox felt a slight itch on his nose, but he resisted the urge to scratch. Chapdelaine picked up a small plate resting in liquid and carefully placed it into the camera.

"Please, sir, remain still," Chapdelaine said, his voice tinged with urgency. "This won't work if you're moving. The photograph will turn out all blurry."

Knox focused on standing still, his breath slow and controlled. He flashed a wide smile. Chapdelaine winced. "No, please. You can't show your teeth. It causes a glare that'll ruin the photograph." Knox straightened up, trying to look serious. Behind the photographer, Norris made faces, doing his best to get Knox to crack. Knox fought the urge and stayed solemn, just as Chapdelaine had asked.

Chapdelaine carefully removed the lens from the camera, adjusting the setup.

"Hold it," Chapdelaine instructed. "Almost done."

Knox remained as still as a statue.

After a few moments, Chapdelaine removed the plate from the camera and placed it into a pan. He then poured water over it from a cup.

"I'm going to need a few more minutes," Chapdelaine said, glancing up at Knox. "You can head back to your cell if you like. I'll bring the photograph to you when I'm finished."

Knox nodded, and Deputy Norris led him out of the room as Chapdelaine continued his work.

Knox and Norris walked down the hallway, heading back to his cell. As they passed by the other inmates, many called out well-wishes, some with pity, others with a quiet respect. Knox soaked it all in, his steps slow, taking his time as he made his way back. The heaviness of the moment pressed down on him, but he couldn't help but feel a strange calm in the chaos.

As they reached the cell, Knox was surprised to find Sheriff Price already inside, standing there, watching him with a serious expression. The sheriff's presence was both familiar and ominous, filling the room in a way that made it feel smaller.

"Good morning, Sheriff!" Knox said, trying to maintain a bit of levity, though the forced cheer in his voice was evident. "How about a game of bluff?"

He reached for the deck of cards, attempting to distract himself, to keep his mind from settling on what was coming.

"Do you have any money left, or did I take it all?" Knox added with a half-hearted smile, his eyes glancing up toward the sheriff, hoping for something, anything to break the tension.

Price stood there, silent for a moment, before his gaze sharpened, cold and firm.

"No cards today, Knox," he said, his voice flat, but there was something in his tone—something that wasn't quite as impassive as he made it sound. "It's almost time. We have a short ride down to Carter's Creek. Are you ready?"

The words hit Knox like a cold gust of wind. He paused, taking a slow breath, the weight of the situation settling in. He turned toward the bottle of wine that had been left for him. Without thinking, he took a long drink from it, feeling the warmth trickle down as it settled in his stomach.

He offered the bottle to Price, holding it out in an almost casual gesture.

Price hesitated, his eyes flicking to the bottle before meeting Knox's gaze. There was a moment of silence, where the sheriff seemed to consider it—long enough that Knox almost thought he wouldn't take it. But the day ahead loomed large, and Price knew what kind of long, difficult hours awaited them.

With a small, reluctant sigh, Price finally took the bottle. He raised it to his lips and took a small, deliberate drink. It was just enough to calm the edge of his nerves but not so much as to dull the responsibility weighing on him. He handed the bottle back to Knox, his eyes never leaving him.

"I'm ready," Knox said quietly, the words almost like a final surrender. He didn't have to say more. "I've made my peace with God."

At that moment, Chapdelaine stepped forward, holding the photograph he had taken earlier. He handed it to Knox, who studied the image for a moment. Seeing himself, fine suit and all, was a strange experience. It was a side of himself he had never seen — nor imagined — until now.

"Will you make sure my momma gets this?" Knox asked, his voice quiet but earnest. He held the photograph out toward Price.

"I will," Price replied. He took the photo from Knox's hands and looked at it briefly before slipping it into his pocket.

"It turned out very nice," Price added after a pause, his words lacking their usual sharpness, as if something in him softened for a brief moment.

"I'm a handsome fella," Knox joked, his lips curling into a smile despite the grim circumstances. But Price didn't return the smile. His face remained as cold and distant as it had been.

The sheriff's gaze shifted briefly, and he gave a small nod.

"Come along," he said, his voice firm but not without an underlying tone of weariness. "Reverend Merry is outside waiting. I told him he could ride with us." Knox followed, his steps slow and deliberate, his mind racing even as he walked in silence. Alongside him, Price and Deputy Norris walked through the narrow corridors of the prison, their footsteps echoing in the empty halls. The cold stone walls seemed to close in on Knox. Finally, they reached an iron door, and Price turned the handle. With a heavy creak, the door opened, leading them out into the yard.

The morning sun cast long, stretching shadows across the dirt, its light sharp against the heavy atmosphere of the day. The air felt thick with tension, each step taken by the group reverberating through the silence of the prison yard.

Reverend Merry, who had been waiting near the gate, noticed them immediately. His face softened with compassion as he rushed over to greet Knox. "I've been praying for you, son," Reverend Merry said, his voice thick with emotion as he placed a hand on Knox's shoulder.

Knox managed a small smile, but it didn't quite reach his eyes. "I'm not scared. It's all going to be alright," he replied, his words more for himself than anyone else.

"That's right. Jesus loves you," Merry affirmed, his voice steady with conviction.

The group moved towards a horse-drawn wagon waiting nearby. The driver nodded at them, and they climbed into the back. As the wagon began to move, Reverend Merry and Knox immediately started to pray, their voices soft but filled with resolve.

As they rode in silence, Deputy Norris glanced over at Sheriff Price, who had been unusually quiet. "John, you alright?" Norris asked, his tone laced with concern, though he knew better than to expect an honest answer.

Price nodded, but there was something in his eyes that spoke of the burden he carried. "Yeah," he muttered. "Just ready for it to be over."

Norris hesitated for a moment before speaking again, his voice quieter this time. "I don't mind cutting the rope. I want you to be able to sleep tonight."

Price met his deputy's gaze, his hardening. "It's part of the job," he said, his voice tired but resolute. "I don't sleep much anyway."

The wagon continued its slow, methodical pace through the streets of town, and with each passing block, the crowd grew larger. People lined the streets, their faces a mix of curiosity, judgment, and something darker—some eager to witness the spectacle of a life coming to an end. Knox could feel their eyes on him. He didn't look at them, though. He kept his eyes fixed straight ahead, trying to hold onto the words Reverend Merry had shared, trying to find peace in the chaos.

As they neared the gallows, the crowd's murmurs grew louder. It was as though the very air was alive with anticipation, and Knox couldn't help but feel a sense of inevitability settle deep inside him. The end was near.

# The Gallows

As the wagon approached the execution site, the air grew thick with the weight of the moment. What had seemed like a quiet, somber journey quickly transformed as the group came upon a spectacle. The scene before them was nothing like the somber spot Knox had expected. Instead, there was a carnival-like atmosphere, with a crowd of ten thousand people filling the hillside overlooking the creek. The people parted as the wagon slowly rolled through, their eyes fixed on the condemned man.

Knox's mouth hung open in disbelief. "Oh my, I didn't know what to expect. But I wasn't expecting all this," he murmured to Reverend Merry, his eyes sweeping across the crowd. He couldn't believe the sheer number of people gathered.

Knox gestured to a man standing off to the side, holding a basket of peaches. "Look over there. That man is selling peaches," he said, his voice tinged with longing. "I'd love to get a big juicy peach."

The sight of the vendor, so mundane and normal in the midst of this chaos, momentarily distracted everyone in the wagon. "Hey Sheriff, can we get some peaches?" Knox asked, a wry smile tugging at his lips.

Price's face remained all business. "Not today, Knox," he replied firmly, keeping his eyes ahead.

Knox shrugged but couldn't help but joke. "How 'bout tomorrow then?" He chuckled. Merry and Deputy Norris couldn't help themselves, each snickering quietly. Price, however, remained silent, his focus fixed on the gallows ahead as the wagon came to a stop.

"Watch your step. Be careful gettin' out," Deputy Norris cautioned, his voice filled with concern.

"Why? You don't want me to break my neck today?" Knox shot back with a grin. His bad joke was met with grimaces from Merry and Norris, but Price remained stone-faced.

With a steady hand, Price helped Knox down from the wagon. As Knox stepped onto the ground, he was met by the eager presence of Scott Singer, the reporter who had been waiting.

"Any last words?" Singer asked excitedly.

Price pushed the reporter back sternly. "Give him some space! This ain't the time for an interview."

Knox looked at the young reporter and gave him a resigned smile. "Ain't got nothing much to say. I'm a guilty man. I wish God's blessings on everyone here today."

A group of uniformed officers stepped forward, pushing the crowd back to give Knox, Price, Norris, and Merry space as they made their way across the field to the gallows, set up near the creek. As they climbed the stairs to the scaffold, Knox's eyes caught sight of Patton Foster nearby.

"May I?" Knox asked, his voice low, but respectful. Price, nodded, allowing him to have a moment. Knox approached Foster, who stood with his arms crossed. The animosity was clear.

"Sir, I'm so sorry," Knox said, his voice thick with regret.

Foster's glare was sharp, his eyes burning with the memory of his sister's murder. There was no forgiveness there, only an unforgiving hardness in his eyes.

"There's nothing I can say that will bring your sister back," Knox continued, his voice breaking, "but I want you to know how sorry I really am."

Foster didn't respond, his expression a mixture of sorrow and anger. It was clear that no words would make a difference.

"Knox, come over here," Sheriff Price called out, his voice stern but calm.

Reluctantly, Knox turned and walked toward the center of the scaffold, where Price and Norris helped position him over the trap door. As they did, Price unlocked the handcuffs, the sound of the metal clicking open a final, haunting reminder of Knox's fate.

"Right here," Price said quietly, pulling the death warrant from his pocket.

"I will now read the death warrant signed by the honorable Judge Jim Quarles," Price continued, his voice strained as he tried to read over the cacophony of the crowd.

"February 21, 1879 - Number 113, State of Tennessee vs. Knox Martin, an indictment for murder came in. The jury empaneled in this case..."

"Louder!" a crowd member shouted, frustration evident.

Price, aggravated, began to shout over the noise.

"Uh... The jury empaneled in this case came here into open court and resumed its consideration, and they aforesaid upon their oath do say that the defendant, Knox Martin, is guilty in manner and form as charged in the bill of indictment of murder in the first degree, and therefore..."

"Louder! We can't hear you!" came another shout from the crowd.

Price, already frazzled, lost his place in the document.

"And thereupon the jury discharged, and the defendant, Knox Martin, being asked whether he had anything further to say why the court should not pronounce his sentence, had nothing to say."

Knox nervously looked around as Price continued reading.

"Um, it is therefore considered by the court, and in accordance with the finding of the jury, it is the judgment of the court that, for the crimes of murder in the first degree, committed by said Knox Martin, on the persons of John and Emily Whittemeyer, in this county on the 16th day of January 1879, as reported to the court by the jury on this day by their verdict, that you, Knox Martin, be taken from this courtroom to the jail of Davidson County, and be delivered to the sheriff of Davidson County, who will keep said Knox Martin safely and securely in said jail until the 28th day of March 1879, when, upon a gallows previously erected, within one mile of this courthouse, he will, between the hours of 10 o'clock a.m. and 2 o'clock p.m., hang the said Knox Martin by the neck until he is dead."

Aunt Mary, who had been pushing her way through the crowd, now stepped forward. Once Price finished reading the death warrant, he held it up for the crowd to see.

"This is the signature of Judge Quarles," Price said.

He leaned over to Reverend Merry, who stood quietly next to Knox.

"Does he have anything he wants to say?" Price asked.

Merry spoke softly into Knox's ear. Knox shook his head. Reverend Merry then pulled out his Bible and began to turn the pages. In the distance, Aunt Mary was still glaring.

"I'm going to read a passage from the 23rd Psalm," Reverend Merry announced.

"The Lord is my shepherd; I shall not want. He maketh me to lie down in green pastures: he leadeth me beside the still waters. He restoreth my soul: he leadeth me in the paths of righteousness for his name's sake. Surely goodness and mercy shall follow me all the days of my life: and I will dwell in the house of the Lord forever."

Merry took Knox's hands in his, and they knelt, praying one final time. Afterward, they both stood. "Goodbye, Knox," Reverend Merry said, his voice cracking slightly.

"Goodbye. Thank you for everything," Knox replied.

"I will pray for you. I am with you. Put your trust in God," Reverend Merry said.

"Yes, sir," Knox replied softly.

Deputy Norris stepped forward and bound Knox's hands behind him, tying his feet tightly together.

"I hope that's not too tight," Norris said, his voice gentle.

"No, sir," Knox responded.

As Norris placed the noose around the gris-gris still wrapped around Knox's neck, he motioned for Price to come closer. The sheriff, holding a hatchet, walked over.

"Goodbye, Mr. Price. Thank you for your kindness. I hope one day we meet again," Knox said, his voice steady but filled with emotion.

Price, his stoic demeanor cracking, fought to maintain composure as he offered a slow nod. He took a step back as Merry rejoined him, and the final preparations were made.

"I'll pray for you," Reverend Merry said softly, his voice thick with emotion. "Remember what I told you."

Knox nodded, his gaze lingering on the sea of faces in the crowd. Their raucous chatter seemed distant now, muffled by the overwhelming dread of what was about to happen. His eyes met Aunt Mary's, cold and unblinking. He offered her a final, faint smile.

Deputy Norris moved to place the hood over Knox's head. But just before he did, he paused, noticing that Knox wasn't directly over the trapdoor.

"Slide over to the left a little," Norris instructed.

With Norris' guidance, Knox shifted, moving to center himself above the trap door. The air felt thick, the tension unbearable, as the final moments drew near.

"He's ready," Deputy Norris said, turning to Sheriff Price.

Price took a long, steadying breath, his eyes locking with Knox's. There was a pause, a lingering moment that stretched too long, before Price finally gritted his teeth and swung the hatchet with all his might. The rope snapped, and the trapdoor beneath Knox opened.

He dropped four feet, his body jerking with the force of the fall. The crowd erupted into a symphony of gasps, cries, and murmurs, their voices blurring into a distant hum against the pounding of Knox's heartbeat in his ears. A woman standing at the foot of the gallows screamed, her voice piercing the air, before she fainted. Knox's body convulsed as it hung there, lifeless yet still caught in the momentum of death. Dr. Summers, noticing the woman collapse, rushed to her side, his focus momentarily diverted from the man at the gallows.

Aunt Mary remained stoic in the crowd, seemingly unfazed by the execution. Sheriff Price, standing at the base of the scaffold, wiped a solitary tear from his eye, struggling to keep his emotions in check.

The convulsions slowly stopped, and Knox's body hung still, his final breath dissolving into the heavy silence that enveloped the crowd.

Once Dr. Summers revived the woman, he hurried forward, his hands shaking with urgency as he reached for Knox's lifeless form.

"Get back!" Sheriff Price barked. Summers hesitated, taking a step back as Price descended the stairs, his boots hitting the wood with a thud.

"You can have him when we're done, but we have to make sure the sentence is carried out," Price continued sharply. "Stay back."

The crowd stood frozen. The silence seemed to stretch on forever. Aunt Mary, without a word, began to fade into the crowd as the people slowly began to disperse, some muttering under their breath, others silent.

"Doctor," Price called, his voice still steady. "Is he dead?"

Dr. Summers stepped forward, checking Knox's pulse with a practiced hand. He looked up at Price, his expression grim.

"He's gone," Dr. Summers confirmed.

Price nodded, the finality of the words settling in. He gave a brief signal to Deputy Norris, who stepped forward, unbinding Knox's hands and legs.

"Be careful with him," Dr. Summers said to his assistant, Bradley Steger, who was standing by, ready to help.

Steger nodded and gently helped Summers remove Knox's body from the gallows. The deputies began to cut the rope, allowing Knox's limp remains to be placed into a waiting coffin.

With reverence, the body was loaded onto a wagon. Summers and Steger climbed into the wagon, ready to transport Knox to an old small shed behind the gallows, where a galvanic battery was waiting.

The scene was quieter now, save for the distant rumble of the wagon wheels as they moved away from the gallows, leaving the crowd behind.

# The Experiment

Summers and Steger carefully carried Knox's lifeless body into the small shed. The air inside was thick with tension, and the smell of damp wood lingered in the stale atmosphere. As they moved toward a wooden table, a group of curiosity seekers, eager to witness the strange experiment, began to gather outside. The growing crowd quickly filled the windows and began pulling at the walls of the shed, trying to peer inside.

"Lay him flat on his back!" Summers ordered, his voice sharp.

Steger and Summers quickly worked together, removing Knox's jacket and shirt. As they did, the gris-gris around his neck caught their attention. They laid his body carefully onto the table, positioning it next to two large glass cylinders with wires hanging from them, the instruments that would hopefully bring him back to life.

"Get his pants!" Summers commanded, his focus unwavering.

Steger ripped Knox's pants off, adjusting his legs as Summers loosened the rope around his throat and carefully reset his broken neck. He massaged the muscles in Knox's neck, attempting to get the blood flowing again.

"Massage his muscles! We have to get the blood circulating! Start with his legs," Summers instructed, his voice taut with urgency.

Steger stuck a thermometer into Knox's mouth as he began rubbing his legs, trying to get his limbs to respond. Summers, equally focused, attached wires to

Knox's heart and temple, monitoring the faint signals in the still body.

"No pulse," Steger announced after a moment, his voice heavy with disappointment.

He checked the thermometer. "His body temperature is 90 degrees."

Summers walked over and placed a hand gently on Knox's forehead. "He's getting cold," he murmured.

He turned back to the glass cylinders, eyes burning with the intensity of his focus. The moment he'd been preparing for had arrived.

"Are you ready?"

Steger, now standing close by, nodded, though his face showed the strain of uncertainty.

Summers pulled out a vial from his coat pocket. He uncorked it, dropped the contents into one of the cylinders. It started to fizz almost immediately. A low humming sound filled the air, followed by a crackling and popping noise that made the hair on Summers' head stand on end.

The room grew tense as the energy built, but then something unexpected happened — the crackling stopped, and the cylinder fell eerily silent.

Steger stepped back, his face pale. "It's not working," he said, his voice trembling.

Time seemed to slow as Summers tapped the cylinder impatiently, his frustration mounting. "I don't know why it's not working!" he exclaimed, anxiety creeping into his tone.

The tension was palpable in the room, the seconds stretching into what felt like hours. Then, suddenly, Knox's face contorted violently. His head jerked back on the table, his eyes bursting open, staring wildly at the ceiling. He gasped for air, his body convulsing as if it had been jolted back into existence. The thermometer fell from his mouth and clattered to the floor.

Steger was frozen, his eyes wide in disbelief as Knox's neck bulged with veins, his eyeballs nearly popping from their sockets. His chest rose and fell as though he were desperate for breath.

"Knox!" Summers cried out, both amazed and frightened. He reached for Knox, trying to understand what was happening.

Steger, still in shock, grabbed Knox's arm and checked for a pulse. The entire cabin shook with the movement of the crowd outside, their voices rising in an excited frenzy. People had climbed onto the roof, tearing away the wood to get a better view of what was happening inside. The noise from outside grew louder, as the crowd erupted in shouts, calling to one another, their voices blending into a chaotic, anxious hum.

"There's a pulse! It's faint, but it's there!" Steger shouted.

But just as quickly, the crackling sound stopped. Knox's body stopped convulsing, and the air in the room became thick with silence.

"Oh no. The battery's dead," Summers muttered in despair.

Steger, not willing to give up, checked again for a pulse. He shook his head, the reality sinking in. Summers started pacing, his mind racing as he scanned the room in frustration.

"We have to make another battery!" Summers exclaimed, his urgency rising.

"We have more zinc sulfate over at the college in Professor Cotham's office," Steger offered quickly.

"Quick! Let's get him back in the coffin," Summers ordered. "We have to get over there. We have no time to waste!"

Together, they scrambled to lift Knox's body back into the coffin, moving quickly but carefully. They hurried toward the door, the urgency of the moment pushing them forward.

♦ ♦ ♦ ♦ ♦ ♦

Sheriff Price along with Deputy Norris and other deputies worked to tear down the gallows. The harsh reality of what had just taken place seemed to hang in the air.

Suddenly, two men, wide-eyed and breathless, rushed toward them. Their faces were flushed with excitement, disbelief etched in every line of their expressions.

"They did it! They brought him back to life!" one of them shouted, his voice thick with amazement.

Price and Norris exchanged a look, their confusion turning to suspicion. What in the world were they talking about?

"He's breathing and has a pulse!" the second man added, his voice shaking with the enormity of what he was saying.

Without another word, Price and Norris sprang into action, their hearts hammering in their chests as they sprinted toward the shed. The crowd seemed to part for them, their shouts of excitement growing louder with each step.

"What's going on? Is he really alive?" Price called out as he and Norris approached the shed.

Nearby, Summers and Steger were hurriedly loading the coffin into a wagon. The urgency in their movements was palpable, their every motion quick and precise as they prepared to leave.

"No time to spare!" Summers called out, his voice tight with tension. "We had him, but the battery died. We have to get to the college!"

With no time to waste, Summers and Steger quickly jumped into the wagon, urging the horse forward. They disappeared down the path, leaving Price and Norris standing there, dumbfounded by what they had just heard.

Scott Singer, the eager reporter, came running over, curiosity written all over his face.

"What's going on? Did they really revive him?" Singer asked, eyes wide with disbelief.

Sheriff Price, still stunned by the news, shook his head in confusion. "I don't know what's going on. He was dead. I watched him die."

With a heavy sigh, Price turned and walked away, his mind racing. Norris followed close behind, offering a polite shrug to the reporter before continuing after the sheriff.

# One More Time

The full moon hung in the sky like an ominous omen, casting its eerie glow on the Nashville Medical College. The three-story Gothic Revival structure loomed like something from a nightmare, its sharp, angular silhouette framed against the dark sky. Summers' wagon creaked and rattled as it approached the imposing building.

Summers and Steger quickly hopped down from the wagon. Summers ran up to the massive door of the building and threw it open. The creak of the door echoed through the silent courtyard like the opening of a tomb. He rushed back to the wagon where Steger was already lifting the coffin, the heavy wood creaking under the weight.

They moved swiftly into the school, their hurried footsteps the only sound in the otherwise eerie silence.

◆ ◆ ◆ ◆ ◆ ◆

The dissection room was lit by a single candle on a table in the corner. The only other source of light came from the pale moonlight filtering in through the window, casting an ethereal glow on the room. The space felt cold and sterile. The air was thick with the scent of old wood and chemicals.

Summers and Steger placed Knox's body carefully on a large table. The two glass cylinders stood on a table beside the body, their wires snaking out like lifelines, ready to challenge mortality.

Steger moved quickly, placing a wire on Knox's forehead.

"No, put that wire on his temple!" Summers snapped, his eyes wide with focus.

Steger's hands were steady, but his eyes betrayed his anxiety as he repositioned the wire. Summers moved to Knox's legs, massaging them as he prepared for the next step.

"Put the other one over his heart!" Summers barked.

Steger swiftly placed the second wire over Knox's chest. Summers, now standing back, started to mix the chemicals in the first cylinder. The silence of the room was suffocating.

"Is it working?" Steger asked, his voice strained. Summers stood back, his impatience mounting. He could feel the weight of the moment pressing on him, the room closing in as the seconds stretched into eternity. His heart raced as he muttered, "Come on! Come on!"

Then, with a deafening roar, the air filled with an eerie crackling sound. The room was flooded with an electrical hum, and Knox's body jerked violently, convulsing in a grotesque semblance of life. The light from the cylinders flickered and pulsed, casting unnatural, twisting shadows across the walls. The noise was unbearable, a storm of raw energy tearing through the space, filling every inch with its deafening intensity.

"I can't stop it!" Summers shouted, his voice rising with shock and fear, as he stumbled back.

Knox's hands clenched into tight fists, his body trembling uncontrollably as it slowly began to lift off the table. A blinding light flooded the room, and the crackling intensified, reverberating through the walls like a living thing.

"Oh my God!" Steger gasped, his voice cracking with disbelief and terror.

Both men recoiled instinctively, their eyes wide with fear, as the crackling energy surged around them. Summers grabbed a nearby chair, lifting it reflexively, as if it could offer protection from the chaotic power now coursing through the air.

"What did we just do?" Summers breathed, his voice a mixture of awe and dread.

The room flashed again with light, and the air thickened with smoke, as if the building itself was alive, pulsing with energy. The flashes quickened, growing brighter and more intense, until, with a violent shattering sound, one of the glass cylinders broke. A piercing scream filled the room, and the intense light that had filled the space faded just as suddenly as it had appeared.

Dr. Summers dropped the chair and shouted, "No!" He staggered back in disbelief. "It can't be!"

Steger, his face pale with fear, began to shout, "Randall!"

Dr. Summers took a step back, his voice trembling. "Oh my, Bradley! You're bleeding!"

As the smoke began to dissipate, Steger's hands trembled as they covered his face. He and Dr. Summers moved cautiously toward the table, their minds struggling to process the unimaginable events unfolding before them.

Dr. Summers leaned over and placed his ear to Knox's chest, his breath shaky. "Is his heart beating?"

Summers pointed toward a nearby table. "Get me the thermometer!"

Still covering his face, Steger shifted slowly to grab the thermometer. Dr. Summers' eyes were wide with disbelief as he whispered, "Knox, can you hear me?"

# "Kansas?"

Scott Singer rode down a long, dusty country road, the sound of his horse's hooves steady against the dirt. The late afternoon sun cast a golden glow over the landscape, and as he neared the imposing figure of a two-story Greek Revival mansion. He guided his horse toward the house, slowing as he neared the side yard where General William Giles Harding stood talking to Robert Green, the head groom, as they examined a horse.

Singer approached them, tipping his hat in a respectful greeting.

"Good afternoon, General," Singer called out, his voice steady and professional. "I'm Scott Singer with the *Tennessean*. I understand you had some trouble with horse thieves a few nights ago. I'm working on a story"

Harding grimaced as he shook his head slowly.

"Yes, that's right. Uncle Bob and the night watchman managed to chase them off."

Uncle Bob, an older African American man with a thick mustache, spoke up, his voice tinged with frustration. "Yeah, I was about to go to bed when I thought I heard some voices out by the barn. Then I heard Reubin, our watchman hollering, so I grabbed my shotgun and ran out to see what was going on. When I got outside, Reubin was pointing towards the field. I fired the gun in the air, and that's when they ran off. Haven't had any trouble since."

Singer nodded thoughtfully, his curiosity piqued. "Did you get a look at them?"

Uncle Bob shook his head, his eyes narrowing at the memory. "It was too dark. Didn't see much of 'em, just shadows."

Singer glanced over and saw a trainer working with several horses, their hooves pounding the dirt in rhythm. Harding followed his gaze and nodded.

"If you've never seen the farm, come along with us. I'll give you a quick tour."

As they began to walk, Singer couldn't help but smile at the thought of the sprawling estate. Harding's conversation drifted into small talk.

"How's business at the *Tennessean*?" Harding asked.

Singer chuckled. "Pretty good… We sold out of the morning paper last Monday. After the hanging of the Bell's Bend killer, the whole town wanted a copy to read about it."

Harding raised an eyebrow, a smirk tugging at his lips. "Ah, yes. I heard they had a crowd. Quite the spectacle, wasn't it?"

Uncle Bob shifted uneasily. "You know," he said, "I saw him…"

Singer stopped mid-step, turning toward him. "Oh? You knew him?"

"No," Uncle Bob muttered, "I didn't know him. But I saw him. The day after he was hanged. I was over watering the horses by the creek, and I saw this black fella walking up the road. He was dressed real nice, suit and all, but he didn't have no shoes. I said good morning, asked him where he was from. He told me he just left Nashville, said his name was Knox Martin. I remember reading about him in the paper. He didn't say much, seemed like he was in a hurry, but he didn't walk too good. Seemed like he was hurt. He walked that way, towards Burn Station."

Harding snickered at the oddity of the story. "Have you been drinking, Bob?" he teased, clearly amused by the strange tale.

Uncle Bob bristled, a flush creeping up his neck. "I swear, General, it was strange. He was dressed all fine, but he didn't have no shoes!"

Singer furrowed his brow, intrigued yet skeptical. He glanced at Harding, but the General was already nudging him forward, eager to continue the tour.

"Come along, let me show you the rest of the place," Harding said with a knowing grin, clearly ready to move on from the conversation.

Uncle Bob ambled off toward the barn, muttering something under his breath, while Harding motioned to the grand mansion, his pride evident as he began to describe the history of the estate.

Still mulling over Uncle Bob's strange account, Singer followed Harding, but his thoughts lingered on the possibility that Knox Martin could still be alive.

◆ ◆ ◆ ◆ ◆ ◆

After touring the grounds and the grand mansion, Singer rode down the road for a few miles, the crisp air biting at his face. He slowed his horse as he came upon a pair of railroad employees clearing brush near the track. Dismounting, Singer approached them with a smile.

"Good afternoon," he called out, tipping his hat. "I have a strange question for you. I'm a reporter for the *Tennessean*, and I'm following up on something someone told me."

Both men paused, giving him a strange look, one of them wiping his brow with the back of his hand.

"Have you seen a black man, wearing a suit, no shoes, walking through here in the past few days?"

One of the workers perked up, his eyes widening at the question. "Man, you ain't gonna believe me," he said, his voice tinged with disbelief. "But the other day, I was relaxing by the river and a guy in a suit, with no shoes on his feet, just like you said, walked down to the water and got a drink. Seemed like he was in a lot of pain. Kept rubbing his neck. I asked him if he was alright. He said they hung him with a rope in Nashville."

Singer tilted his head, intrigued. The second worker gave a surprised laugh. "Ain't no way," he said, shaking his head.

The first man continued, undeterred. "I thought he was joking, but he showed me his neck. It was raw, like he had a rope wrapped around it. I asked him where he was headed, and he said Kansas."

Singer's curiosity deepened, his pen poised in his pocket. "How old was he?"

"Probably in his twenties. A fairly young man," the worker replied.

"Which way did he go?" Singer pressed, his eyes fixed on the man.

The worker pointed past the brush and toward the horizon. "He went down yonder, following the road west. I reckon that's the way to Kansas."

Singer nodded, thanking the men for their time. He climbed back onto his horse, his mind racing. As he turned his horse toward Nashville, the sky darkening ahead, his thoughts lingered on the strange tale. Was it possible that Knox Martin had survived the execution?

Did the doctors successfully resurrect him? And if so, what was he doing, walking towards Kansas? The questions only multiplied.

◆ ◆ ◆ ◆ ◆ ◆

The next day in the newspaper office, Scott Singer sat at his typewriter, the clacking of the keys filling the otherwise quiet room as he pounded out his latest story. The noise stopped momentarily as Lance Balogh, the short, balding editor, walked past, casting a quick glance over Singer's shoulder.

"What are you thinking? We can't print that!" Balogh's voice was filled with surprise and disapproval.

Singer didn't flinch, his fingers pausing just long enough to look up. "Sir, I have firsthand accounts from two people near the Harding farm who swear they saw a black man matching Knox Martin's description. Both said he was headed west, toward Burns Station, on foot. One of the witnesses asked him where he was going..."

Singer hesitated for a moment, letting the suspense build before he added, "He said Kansas."

Balogh let out a sharp, incredulous laugh. "Kansas? You're serious, aren't you?"

Singer nodded earnestly, his expression unwavering. He was certain about his sources and their accounts.

Balogh shook his head slowly, his amusement fading into a resigned frustration. "Alright, if you have two sources, I'll let you run with it. But it ain't going on the front page. You got me?"

"Understood," Singer replied, his voice steady, already moving back to the typewriter.

Balogh's expression softened slightly. "Tell you what... Why don't you go talk to the doctors who experimented on that young man? See what they have to say."

"Yes, sir," Singer responded, his fingers returning to the keys. "I'll get on it."

♦ ♦ ♦ ♦ ♦ ♦

In the bright, sunlit dissecting room of the Nashville Medical College, Bradley Steger, a bandage covering his right eye, was carefully working on a cadaver while Dr. Summers stood by, observing. The room, bathed in natural light streaming through large windows, had an almost surreal quality to it. The scent of formaldehyde hung in the air, sharp and sterile. Despite the warmth and brightness of the day outside, an eerie calm pervaded the room.

The door opened, and Scott Singer walked in, his eyes widening as he took in the scene before him. Upon spotting the lifeless body on the table, he froze.

"Good morning, gentlemen," Singer said, his voice faltering as his eyes moved from the cadaver to the doctors.

Both doctors chuckled, clearly unfazed by the gruesome sight. Singer's gaze moved to Steger's bandaged eye, curiosity piqued.

"Sir, if I may ask, what happened to your eye?" he inquired.

Steger shot him an annoyed glance, but Dr. Summers quickly answered.

"There was an incident a few days ago," he said. "There was a, uh... We had an accident during an experiment. My colleague here caught some glass in his eye."

Steger nodded, his expression stiff.

"Can I help you with something?" Dr. Summers asked politely.

Singer gathered his composure and, with some hesitation, walked past the cadaver to approach Summers.

"Yes, I am Scott Singer with the *Tennessean*. You are the doctors who were present at Knox Martin's execution, correct?"

"Yes, we were there." Summers replied coyly.

"What happened?" Singer asked, his curiosity piqued.

Steger shot a quick, wary glance at Summers, but Summers simply smiled. "You mean after the execution?"

Steger shifted uneasily, growing visibly nervous.

"Mister, we are right in the middle of —"

Before Steger could finish, Summers cut him off with a wave of his hand, signaling him to be quiet. "I can assure you that the experiments we conducted were cleared by the sheriff's office and approved by the deceased before he was hanged. I made sure that he was compensated handsomely for his contributions to science," he said, his words steady and professional.

Singer leaned in, his frustration building. "So, what happened?"

Steger glanced around nervously, clearly uncomfortable with the direction the conversation was heading. Summers remained calm.

"You want to know if we revived Mr. Martin?" Summers asked, his voice lowering, as though inviting

Singer into a secret world.

"Yes, sir," Singer replied. "There are reports of him walking west. It's believed he might be headed to Kansas."

Summers raised an eyebrow. "Kansas? I thought that he was from Alabama. Wouldn't he be going back there?"

"I don't know," Singer answered, his voice tinged with confusion. "Maybe he thought he could get a fresh start out west."

Summers's expression remained inscrutable. "I am not at liberty to speak of what happened during our experiments. But one day in the future, I intend to publish them in a journal."

Singer's patience was wearing thin. "We did have some degree of success," Summers continued, his tone becoming more distant. "But there were unexpected difficulties as well. It was a day I will not soon forget."

As Summers spoke, Steger returned to his dissection, clearly uninterested in continuing the conversation. Summers, however, walked over to his desk, the creak of the old wooden floorboards the only sound in the otherwise quiet room.

"Let me show you something," Summers said, the words almost hesitant. "I got a letter yesterday."

Steger froze, his hands pausing over the cadaver as he turned to face Summers. His surprise was palpable.

"You're going to show it to him?" Steger asked.

Summers didn't answer immediately. Instead, he reached into the drawer of his desk and pulled out a letter. He adjusted his glasses before carefully unfolding the letter and beginning to read aloud.

"Dr. Summers, I hear you were one of the

resurrectors of the man that was hung in Nashville last week. I want to ask you something about him."

Singer raised an eyebrow as Summers continued reading.

"Yesterday, a black man passed through here giving his name as Knox Martin, and said he was hung in Nashville and was afterwards brought back to life by the doctors, and that he was then on his way to Jackson County, where he used to live."

Singer's jaw dropped.
"Is this Knox Martin alive or dead? Please write and let me know. There is some excitement here about him. I am not satisfied so I ask you to write. Direct your letter to me at Winchester, Tennessee, as I will be there next week. Respectfully, James Mason."

Singer stood in stunned silence, his jaw practically hanging open as he processed the contents of the letter. Steger, on the other hand, was visibly irritated.

"May I?" Singer finally asked, his hand outstretched toward Summers.

Summers handed him the letter without a word, and the young reporter's eyes raced across the page, trying to absorb the incredible claim made by James Mason. He shook his head, still in disbelief.

"Doctor Summers," Singer said, his voice unsteady, "if I can get permission from the editor, may I print this letter in tomorrow's paper?"

Summers paused, the faintest glint of hesitation in his eyes, but it quickly faded. Steger's gaze, meanwhile, remained a steady, piercing glare, aimed directly at Summers, as if silently warning him.

"I would not object," Summers replied, his voice calm, almost too calm.

Singer's excitement was palpable, his words tumbling out without thought. "Did you really bring him back to life?"

Summers flashed a brilliant, almost unsettling smile. "Dr. Steger and I need to get back to work. Thank you for stopping by."

Singer's excitement was barely contained as he walked toward the door, but he stopped in his tracks when Summers called his name.

"Oh, Mr. Singer…" Summers said, his tone now quieter but still holding that same air of mystery.

Singer turned around, his face full of anticipation.

"Please call on us again if you locate Mr. Martin," Summers said, his voice almost playful.

Steger, still glaring at Summers, didn't move or speak. Singer nodded eagerly, his mind already racing with the possibilities of the story.

"Yes, sir. If he is out there I'll find him!" he said, before rushing out of the room, the door slamming behind him.

◆ ◆ ◆ ◆ ◆ ◆

An hour later, Scott Singer walked into the newspaper office, still lost in his thoughts after his visit with the doctors. As he stepped inside, he noticed a familiar looking man sitting in a chair, holding a package. Lance Balogh, almost giddy, rushed over to him with excitement written across his face.

"Scott, you have a visitor," Balogh said, pointing to the man waiting.

Singer walked over, his curiosity piqued. The individual looked vaguely familiar, but he couldn't place him right away.

"Hi, can I help you with something?" Singer asked, offering a polite smile.

The man stood up and extended his hand. Singer shook it, still trying to place him.

"I'm Josiah Taylor. I was the attorney for Knox Martin in the Bell's Bend murder case," Taylor said.

A light bulb went off in Singer's mind.

"That's right. I knew you looked familiar," Singer replied, finally recognizing him.

"I need to show you something," Taylor said, his voice tinged with seriousness.

Taylor carefully opened the package in his hands, revealing a piece of rope. He held it up for Singer to see.

"I think this was part of the rope that they used to hang Knox," Taylor said quietly.

Singer frowned, confusion washing over him. "What do you mean? Why do you think that?"

Taylor reached into the package again, pulling out a photograph of Knox. Singer's eyes widened.

"This is Knox Martin. How did you get this?" he asked, bewildered.

"It says here on the package that it was sent from Montgomery, Alabama," Taylor explained.

Singer's mind raced. He couldn't quite grasp what was happening.

"I don't understand what's going on. One of the deputies told me that they took a photograph in the jail before Knox was executed. Why did he send it to you?" Singer asked, trying to make sense of it all.

Taylor looked thoughtful for a moment. "Maybe he believes that I'm the reason he lost his case. Maybe he wants me to know that he cheated death. I can't figure it out."

Singer's expression was one of frustration. "It doesn't make sense."

He sat down, his mind spinning as the three of them sat in silence, unable to make sense of the strange turn of events.

Balogh, sensing the need to act, spoke up. "Why don't you go find the sheriff and talk to him? He needs to see this."

Singer nodded. He turned to Taylor. "Can I borrow these?"

"Of course," he said, handing over the rope and the photograph.

Singer left the office, contemplating the mystery. Balogh turned to a reporter at a nearby desk.

"I know this sounds crazy," Balogh began, "but I want you to go talk to some of the lawyers at the courthouse. See if there is some kind of statute about prisoners being brought back to life after they are executed."

The reporter hopped up and walked out the door, eager to begin the search for answers.

A little while later, Singer walked through the courthouse, scanning the crowd for anyone who might help him make sense of this bizarre situation. His eyes landed on Deputy Norris, and he made his way toward him.

"Deputy!" Singer called, waving the photograph in his hand.

Norris walked over, his steps purposeful. "Yes, sir. Can I help you?"

Singer pulled the photograph from his pocket, holding it out for Norris to see. "Do you recognize this?"

Norris was taken aback, his surprise evident on his face. "Where did you get that?"

"It was mailed to Knox Martin's attorney," Singer replied.

Norris's eyes nearly popped out of his head as he stared at the photograph. "Has the sheriff seen this?"

Singer shook his head. "No."

"Come with me," Norris said urgently. He motioned for Singer to follow him.

Norris and Singer walked down the hall until they came to an office. There they found Sheriff Price sitting in a chair, reading the morning newspaper. His usual stern demeanor was interrupted as he glanced up at the two men.

"Deputy," Price muttered, lowering the paper. "What is it now?"

"Sheriff, the reporter has something to show you," Norris replied.

Singer pulled the photograph from his coat pocket and handed it to Price. The sheriff's eyes narrowed with growing anger as he looked it over.

"Where'd you get this?" Price demanded, his voice rising. "You fooling with me?"

Price grabbed the photograph from Singer's hand, inspecting it carefully.

"It was sent from Montgomery, Alabama, to Knox Martin's attorney," Singer explained, trying to remain calm.

Price's face twisted in disbelief. "I mailed this to Knox's mother the day after we hung him," he said, his voice thick with confusion. "This is impossible."

He paused, his mind working through the impossible scenario.

"She lived in Montgomery," he added, his voice softening as if trying to grasp the truth of it.

"There's more," Singer said, pushing forward. "There was also a piece of rope in the package."

Singer handed the rope to Price, who studied it carefully. The sheriff's brow furrowed deeper.

"Norris," Price muttered, his voice almost a growl. "You're the one who put it around his neck. What do you think?"

Norris took the rope, inspecting it closely. "It sure looks like the rope we used," he said, his tone steady, though his voice carried a trace of doubt.

Price and Norris exchanged glances, both men caught in the whirlwind of disbelief.

"Come on," Price finally said, breaking the silence. "Let's go show Judge Quarles."

The three men moved quickly, heading down the hall to the judge's chambers.

Sheriff Price burst through the door, followed by Norris and Singer. Judge Quarles looked up from his desk, clearly frustrated.

"Damnit, John," Quarles grumbled. "Can't you see I'm busy?"

But Price was determined, pushing past the usual pleasantries.

"This can't wait," Price said urgently.

He slammed the rope and the photograph onto Quarles' desk, the impact loud in the otherwise quiet room. Quarles glanced at the items, his irritation turning to confusion.

"Let me ask you something," Price continued, his voice tense. "What would happen if a doctor was able to bring Knox Martin back to life?"

Judge Quarles scratched his head, scanning the photograph and rope with a perplexed expression.

"Well, my decision was that he was to be hanged by the neck until he was dead," Quarles said, his voice heavy with uncertainty. "What's going on?"

Singer stepped forward, his voice low but firm. "Those doctors at the medical school may have brought him back."

Quarles' face went pale, his shock palpable. "That's impossible," he whispered, his eyes widening as the full weight of the statement hit him.

"I don't understand it either," Price muttered, his voice a mix of frustration and disbelief.

Quarles paused, his fingers tapping the edge of the desk as he processed the implications of what they were saying.

"Well, I—uh, this is unprecedented," Quarles finally said, shaking his head slowly. "If they did bring him back, I suppose he's a free man."

The words hung in the air like a heavy fog, each man caught in the surreal gravity of the situation.

Norris, Price, and Singer stepped out of the judge's office, the door creaking as it closed behind them. The hallway was dimly lit, but through the tall windows, they could see the vibrant orange and pink hues of the setting sun casting long shadows across downtown Nashville.

As they walked down the hallway, Price's eyes wandered to one of the windows. In the distance, on a dirt road stretching into the horizon, the silhouette of a man could be seen walking into the blinding rays of the sun. For a moment, Price squinted, trying to make out the figure. The man's form was barely more than a shadow against the blazing sky, his steps steady, determined.

"Do you really think those doctors really resurrected him?" Price asked, his voice low, almost uncertain.

Scott Singer paused before answering, his mind running through the facts, weighing every angle. "Logically, I have to say no," he said after a moment, his voice tinged with doubt. "But in reality, I have no idea. What do you think?"

Price looked out the window again. He seemed to be contemplating the impossible, trying to understand how a man once condemned to die could have found his way back. "He deserved to die for what he did," Price finally muttered, his words heavy. "But if Knox did get a second chance... I hope things turn out the right way for him."

# "We'll See Him Again"

The next morning, Sheriff Price didn't go to the station. He left his badge on the kitchen table and walked down 10th Avenue until he reached the white clapboard walls of the First Baptist Church. The bell had already rung, and the last hymn was drifting out through the windows in low, mournful waves.

He hesitated before pushing the door open.

Inside, heads turned.

He knew what they saw: the white man who hanged Knox Martin on the gallows.

The stares weren't angry—just tight, uneasy, watchful. Price kept his eyes on the floor and slid into the back pew, hands folded, hat resting beside him.

He sat like a shadow, unmoving, listening.

Reverend Nelson Merry stood at the pulpit, one hand on his Bible, the other raised toward the ceiling.

The name Knox Martin hadn't been spoken aloud in the chapel since the verdict—not by the deacons, not from the pews. But today, it hovered in the air, waiting.

"He that believeth and is baptized shall be saved," Merry said, his voice calm but resolute. "But he that believeth not shall be damned."

He paused, letting the words settle in the wood and bone of the room.

"Some of you were there. Some of you heard the news... or read about it. And I know many of you wondered why I went into that jail, why I laid hands on a man the state had already condemned."

He looked out at them—not accusing, not pleading, just telling Knox's story.

"It wasn't for pity. It wasn't even for justice. It was for mercy. Because even the man who waits for the gallows can be reached by grace."

A few murmurs—barely audible—rose from the back.

"He confessed to me. He wept in that cell. And when he asked to be baptized, I did not hesitate. Not because I knew what was in his heart, but because the Lord did."

Merry closed his Bible, slowly, gently.

"Knox Martin died without a headstone, without a service, without a hymn sung over his body. But don't let that fool you. His soul left that jail covered in the blood of the Lamb. And the Lord, not man, will decide what to do with him next."

From the back pew, Sheriff Price shifted in his seat.

When the service ended, and the crowd began to file out, Price remained behind.

Reverend Merry stepped down from the altar and approached the sheriff with a quiet kindness in his eyes.

"I wondered if I'd see you," Merry said, offering a hand. "You've been on my heart."

Price stood slowly. He took the reverend's hand and shook it but said nothing.

"I've been praying for you," Merry continued. "What you had to do... It's a tough job."

Price's voice was low. "I thought maybe it'd feel like closure. Like something was over. But it ain't."

Merry nodded. "It rarely is."

They stood a moment in the quiet, the chapel empty now except for the two of them.

"Don't carry more than you were meant to," Merry said softly. "The Lord forgave him. And that means you can forgive yourself, too."

Price looked away, out through the stained-glass panes, where the spring light broke into a kaleidoscope of color.

Merry continued, "We'll see him again."

The sheriff raised an eyebrow, his mind racing back to the reports of Knox being alive.

Reverend Merry's smile was gentle, but his eyes held a depth of knowledge. "If he truly meant that prayer he prayed with me in the jail, the Bible says we'll see him face to face — Not as he was. But as he was meant to be..."

The sheriff gave a nod and put his hat back on.

"Take care, Reverend."

"And you," Merry replied.

Price stepped out into the street, where the sun was beginning its climb, the streets waking up around him.

◆ ◆ ◆ ◆ ◆ ◆

The quiet crackle of the fire was the only sound that filled Aunt Mary's small cabin. The flames danced in the hearth, casting flickering shadows across the room. Outside, the night was pitch black, the moon hidden behind thick clouds, leaving the cabin cloaked in darkness, save for the soft, warm glow of the fire.

Aunt Mary sat in her old rocking chair, her weathered hands resting on her lap as she stared into the fire, her thoughts a maze of memories and unspoken words.

Her eyes shifted to the newspaper in her hands. The headline caught her eye: "*IS KNOX MARTIN ALIVE?*" Her lips parted slightly, and for a moment, she simply stared at the words.

With a slow, deliberate motion, Aunt Mary stood up from her chair. The soft creak of the wooden floor echoed as she shuffled across the room, the shadows following her every step. She approached a small table near the back of the room, where a shrine sat — humble, but heavy with significance. It was adorned with candles, trinkets, and tokens that told stories of faith, mystery, and protection.

Aunt Mary reached out, her fingers brushing the edges of the cloth doll sitting at the center of the shrine. The doll's features were eerily similar to Knox's, down to the tiniest details — a representation of her faith, her love, and her unwavering belief that he would be defended by her dark magic. She lifted the doll carefully, holding it up to the dim firelight. A mysterious smile played at the corners of her lips, a knowing look in her eyes as she whispered softly, almost to herself.

"My boy, I told you that you was protected."

The sanctuary of the First Baptist Church was empty, save for the flicker of a single candle.

Night pressed against the stained-glass windows, black and heavy.

Reverend Merry sat in the front pew, head bowed. After a long moment, he lifted his eyes.

"Amen."

He reached into his pocket and withdrew a small bundle — threadbare, feathered, faded.

The gris-gris.

He turned it over once. Then again.

With a soft sigh, he rose and stepped to the altar where the candle burned low.

He whispered, "Put away the strange gods that are among you..."

Then, slowly, he held the charm over the flame.

The twine hissed.

Smoke rose — thin, bitter, and quick to vanish.

He watched until it was gone.

The candle shuddered once, then steadied.

The sanctuary was silent again.

# Author's Note

Was Knox Martin resurrected?

What we know is this: he was hanged before a crowd of thousands in 1879… and yet, days later, rumors began to spread that he had risen from the dead.

The story begins on January 14, 1879, when Patton Foster visited the small log cabin of his sister Emily Whittemeyer and her husband John, near Bell's Bend in West Nashville. No one answered the door—but inside, he heard the faint cries of his infant nephew.

When Patton stepped inside, he found a scene of horror. Emily and John lay dead in their bed, bludgeoned beyond recognition. John's eye socket had been crushed. Emily's face was shattered. And crawling on top of her lifeless body was their 18-month-old child, desperate to nurse.

Two of John's coats and his wallet were missing. A ferry operator reported seeing a man named Knox Martin, a day laborer who had been helping the Whittemeyers, crossing the river wearing a black coat that matched John's.

Knox Martin, a former slave from Alabama, was arrested shortly after. He confessed to the murders, explaining that John had refused to pay him for his work. But there was another detail that caught the attention of authorities and the press.

Martin was known to have been close with a woman named Aunt Mary—a voodoo practitioner and midwife in the African American community. Days before the murders, Martin had visited Aunt Mary, seeking her advice and spiritual protection. Some whispered she had given him charms. Others claimed she had given him something much stronger.

Martin was found guilty and sentenced to hang on March 28, 1879.

That afternoon, Sheriff John L. Price led Knox Martin through the streets of Nashville toward the gallows. Over ten thousand people gathered to watch. Among them were Dr. Summers and Dr. Steger, local physicians deeply fascinated by galvanism—the belief that electricity could reanimate the dead. Influenced by Mary Shelley's *Frankenstein* and real experiments in Europe, they approached Knox in his cell and made him an offer: allow them to attempt resuscitation after the execution.

With nothing left to lose, Knox agreed.

When the trapdoor was released, Martin dropped and died within minutes. But Sheriff Price insisted his body remain hanging for the full fifteen minutes. Finally, the doctors were allowed to retrieve the body. They gently realigned Knox's neck, placed him in a wooden coffin, and carried him to a nearby cabin.

There, the doctors went to work. They massaged his limbs, connected electrodes to his chest and head, and activated a battery.

To their astonishment, Knox Martin's eyes opened. He gasped for air. His chest rose and fell.

And then… it stopped.

The battery had drained. His pulse faded again. The doctors declared him dead—again.

Still determined, the physicians moved Martin's body to the Literary Building on College Hill, where a second attempt was made in secret. No press was allowed. No official statement was ever given. The doctors refused to speak of what happened.

Then the rumors began.

Reports spread through Nashville's African American community that Knox Martin had survived—that he had escaped death. Some claimed he was headed to Kansas. Others believed he returned to Alabama.

A letter published in *The Tennessean* from a farmer in Madison County, Alabama, claimed a man calling himself Knox Martin had recently passed through. He said he had been hanged, revived by doctors, and was now heading for Jackson County, where his family once lived.

Two days later, the President of the Nashville Savings Bank received a package from Montgomery. Inside: a photograph of Knox Martin… and a piece of rope, believed to be from the gallows.

After that, the trail went cold.

Some believe Knox was quietly buried in an unmarked grave in Mount Olivet Cemetery. Others claim he escaped and lived out his life under a new name. Still others say his spirit—charged by electricity and bound by voodoo—never rested at all.

They say it lingers still in Lindsley Hall, where the second resurrection was attempted behind locked doors.

Is Knox Martin dead or alive?

History never gave a clear answer.

For more information on the Knox Martin story, check out *Southern Ghost Stories: South Nashville*.

www.ingramcontent.com/pod-product-compliance
Lightning Source LLC
Chambersburg PA
CBHW071122100726
47908CB00008B/2462